THE GREAT BEAR

BOOK TWO OF **THE MISEWA SAGA**

THE GREAT BEAR

DAVID A. ROBERTSON

PUFFIN
an imprint of Tundra Book Group,
a division of Penguin Random House Limited

First published in hardcover by Puffin Canada, 2021
Published in this edition, 2022

1 2 3 4 5 6 7 8 9 10

The author would like to acknowledge the
Canada Council for the Arts for their support.

Manufactured in Canada

Library and Archives Canada Cataloguing in Publication

Title: The Great Bear / David A. Robertson.
Names: Robertson, David, 1977- author.
Series: Robertson, David, 1977- Misewa saga ; bk. 2.
Description: Series statement: The Misewa saga ; Book two
Identifiers: Canadiana 20220180601 | ISBN 9780735266155 (softcover)
Subjects: LCGFT: Fantasy fiction. | LCGFT: Time-travel fiction. | LCGFT: Novels.
Classification: LCC PS8585.O32115 G74 2022 | DDC jC813/.6—dc23

Library of Congress Control Number: 2020951757

www.penguinrandomhouse.ca

For Emily, Cole, Anna, Lauren, and James

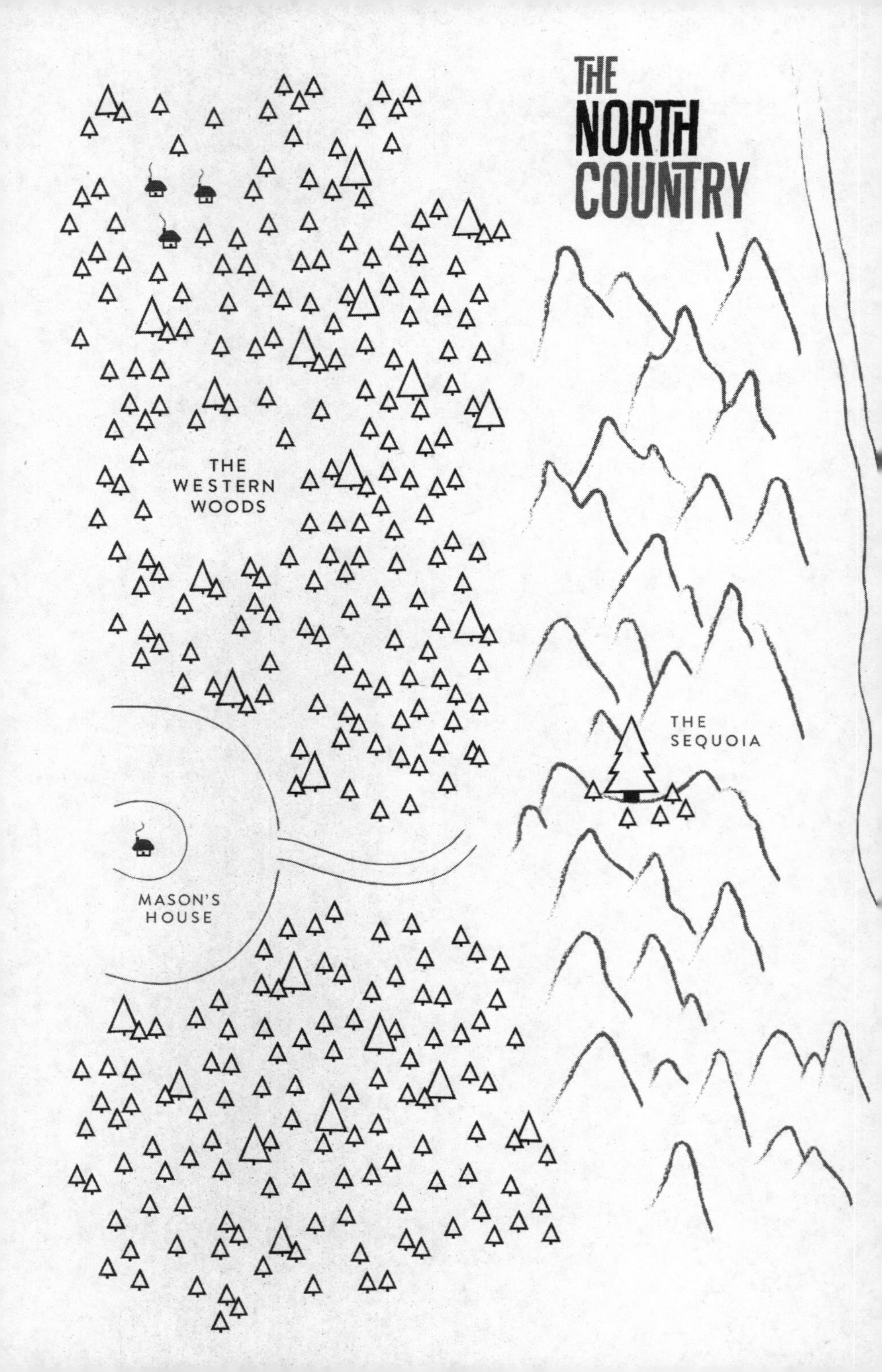
THE NORTH COUNTRY
THE WESTERN WOODS
THE SEQUOIA
MASON'S HOUSE

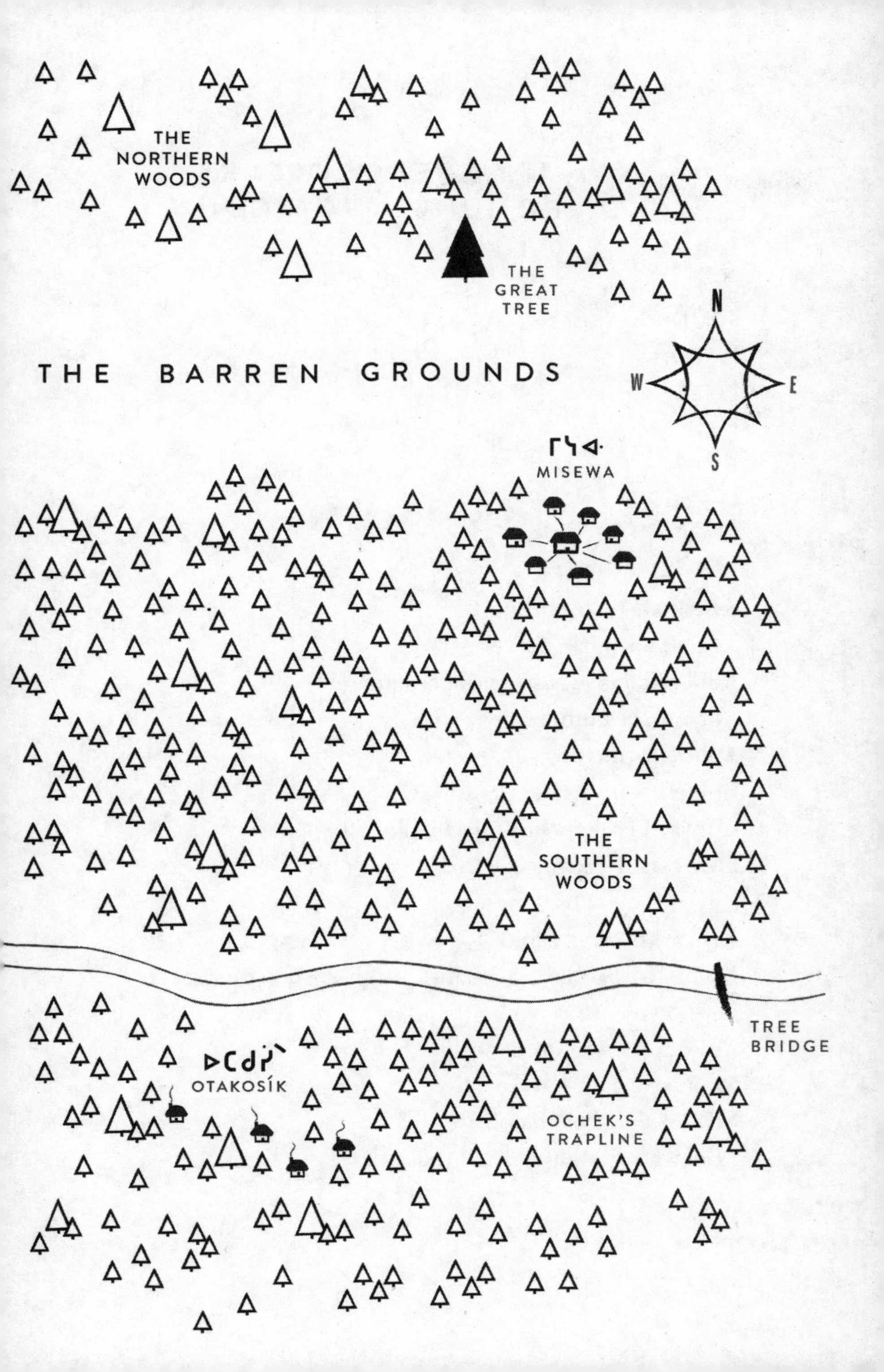
THE NORTHERN WOODS
THE GREAT TREE
N
W
E
S
THE BARREN GROUNDS
ᒥᓭᐘ
MISEWA
THE SOUTHERN WOODS
TREE BRIDGE
ᐅᑕᑯᓰᐠ
OTAKOSÍK
OCHEK'S TRAPLINE

SWAMPY CREE GLOSSARY AND PRONUNCIATION GUIDE

SOUNDS:

É – ay

Í – ee

I – ih

A – ah

O – oh

E – eh

Ahtik ah-tick: caribou
Amisk ah-misk: beaver
Arikwachas eric-watch-ahs: squirrel
Astum ah-stum: come
Atim ah-tim: dog
Ehe eh-heh: yes
Ekosani eh-koh-sah-nih: thank you
Iskwésis ih-skway-sis: girl
Kayas k-eye-ahs: long ago
Kihiw kih-ewe: eagle
Kiskisitotaso kih-skih-sih-toh-tah-so: don't forget about who you are
Kókom koo-kuhm: grandmother
Makésiw mah-kay-soo: fox
Mihko mih-koh: blood
Misewa miss-ah-waa: all that is

Miskinahk miss-kih-nack: turtle
Mistapew miss-ta-pay-oh: big foot (giant)
Moshom moo-shum: grandfather
Muskwa muh-skwa: bear
Nikamon nih-kah-mawn: a song
Nimama nih-mah-mah: my mother
Nipapa nih-pah-pah: my father
Niska nih-ska: goose
Nitanis nih-tan-iss: my daughter
Níwakomakanak nee-wack-oh-mah-kah-nack: my relatives
Ochek oh-check: fisher
Ochekatchakosuk oh-check-ah-chack-oh-suhk: the fisher stars
Oho oh-ho: owl
Otakosík oh-tack-oh-seek: yesterday
Pinésíwan pih-nay-see-wahn: it is thundering
Pipisché pih-pihs-chay: robin
Pisiskowak pih-sis-koh-wack: animals
Pos pohs: cat
Tahtakiw tah-ta-koo: crane
Tansi tan-sih: hello
Wapistan wah-pihs-tawn: marten
Yapéw ya-pay-ewe: bull moose

ONE

Morgan raised a crude, homemade slingshot she had made herself. She pulled back the round stone, the elastic stretching all the way to her face, and took aim at a prairie chicken. The orange-throated bird, with its striped, round body, was pecking at the ground for seeds and insects. It was completely oblivious to the presence of Morgan, Eli, and Arik, who was usually a rather loud squirrel but managed to stay quiet when on the hunt. Morgan's hands were trembling. It made her cheek tremble, her vision shaky. She lowered the slingshot.

She whispered to Eli, "Didn't you kill the exact same kind of bird, with this exact weapon, but when you were, like, in kindergarten?"

"I did it when I was learning," Eli whispered in response. "Age doesn't matter."

"That doesn't answer my question."

"If I can interject," Arik said, also whispering. "If I couldn't just sprint after the bird and kill it, I would totally use a slingshot."

"I feel like kids use slingshots because they aren't old enough to use an *actual* weapon," Morgan said. "Like Bart Simpson. He uses a slingshot, doesn't he?"

"Who's Bart Simpson?" Arik asked.

"He's a cartoon character on earth," Eli explained, rolling his eyes at Morgan.

"What's a cartoon character?"

"*Heeere* we go." Morgan sat down, and the others sat with her, in the woods just south of Misewa, in the middle of summer. Eli and Morgan were wearing Misewa clothing, made for them by villagers after their first journey to the North Country. When not on Askí, they stashed them in a sack that they hung from a tiny burl on the Great Tree, which contained the portal through which they always came to the Barren Grounds. The sack held two options for each sibling—a warm outfit and a cool one—to clothe them for all seasons.

"You know how Eli draws stuff?" Morgan began.

"Yes, of course." Arik nodded. "That's how you travel here."

"Right, okay." They were getting somewhere. "So, on earth, people can make drawings seem alive. Like, they move and stuff. They become *animated*."

"Sooo . . . some people can make drawings walk around on earth? Like, if the drawings on the Council Hut jumped off the walls and started dancing around?" Arik asked. "*Wizards!*"

"No!" Then Morgan clapped a hand over her mouth and glanced over at the prairie chicken to see if it was still there.

It was pecking away. "No," she corrected herself, whispering once more. "They don't . . ." She rubbed her face out of frustration. "They don't come alive. They just . . . move around on a screen. A screen that's kind of like, I don't know, glass paper." Morgan had tried to think of a way to explain it without complicating the matter. She wasn't certain she'd succeeded. "And they're in made-up stories. They're fake."

After a moment of thought, Arik shrugged. "That sounds dumb."

"Some of them are dumb," Eli said. "But anyway, slingshots aren't just for kids."

"Yeah, well . . ." Morgan got up on her knees and turned towards the prairie chicken again. She raised the slingshot and took aim. "Let's just call it learning and pretend that we never had this conversation. I'm cool with using a slingshot."

She took a deep, calming breath, trying her best to ward off shaky hands, shaky cheeks, and shaky vision. She would never hit the bird like that. She had the leather pocket pinched firmly between her thumb and index finger, ready to let the stone fly towards the target.

Morgan heard a huff behind her.

"It's not like I haven't shown you a *million* things since you've been living in Misewa," Arik grumbled, loudly enough for Morgan to hear.

The volume of her grumbling, like the huff, seemed deliberate. The slingshot was lowered once more. Morgan craned her neck around to see Arik still sitting, leaning against a tree, her arms crossed, looking away from Morgan.

"Arik," Morgan said. "Come on."

"I believe, if I'm not mistaken, I walked you through the making of a certain slingshot."

Morgan crouched in front of Arik, put her hand under the animal being's furry chin, and made Arik look at her.

"I'm sorry, okay?" Morgan said. "Next time we come, I'll bring an iPad and show you some cartoons."

"Really?" Arik perked up.

"Yes, really." Morgan got back into position; the prairie chicken had not moved much at all. "But just one time, because, back on earth, all the kids ever do is stare at their screens. They never do things like this. Neither do the adults, for that matter. Adults are maybe even worse."

"They just sit there and stare at these iPad things?" Arik said.

Morgan raised her slingshot and took aim. "They'll literally play a game like this and never do something like this *actually*. I was like that too, up until two weeks ago." She corrected herself then, and did what she'd come to call Misewa Math, calculating that one hour of earth time equaled one week of time on Askí. "Well, two weeks *earth* time. It's been, like, a little over two years that we've spent here."

"That's so confusing," Arik said.

"Yeah, I know."

"*I* wasn't staring at a screen," Eli said. "I always did stuff like this."

"Yes, Eli, I know." Morgan sighed. "But I was kind of busy playing musical foster homes."

"Sorry."

"It's fine."

"Well, I think these iPads sound pretty silly," Arik said.

"I mean . . ." But Morgan let her thought trail off. There'd be time to discuss the benefits and drawbacks of technology over dinner.

She took another breath. She had never killed anything before, and she was sure that was the cause of her shakiness. She told herself that it was just as Eli had said many times: hunting was the way of life for many Indigenous people, and the way of life for beings in Misewa. The villagers were still gathering strength, still recovering from the countless years they'd spent in the White Time. If they didn't catch four-legged and two-legged things, they would go hungry. And they'd been hungry for too long. So Morgan took one more deep breath, let it out slowly, and released the stone, straight and true.

TWO

Misewa held a feast that night to honor Morgan's accomplishment of killing the prairie chicken. The entire village gathered in front of the Council Hut, sitting on the grass around a blanket upon which the food was spread out. There were berries, bannock (better than any bannock Morgan had tasted on earth), fish, venison, hare, and, of course, the prairie chicken, of which each villager received a small portion.

On Morgan and Eli's first visit to Misewa, the prairie chicken would have been an important catch, a meal that would have satisfied everyone in the small village, even in very modest portions. There was so little food in that time of famine.

The animal beings had enough to eat now, and eat they did, but just enough and never more. They would never fall into the sort of greed they had observed in Mason, the man who had stolen the summer birds. They ate only their fill, and kept stores of food for the White Time.

But there were simply too many mouths in Misewa now for one prairie chicken to feed. It was no longer just Chief and Council—Muskwa, the bear; Oho, the owl; and Miskinahk, the turtle—and the small population of villagers: a caribou, two foxes, a beaver, a bison, a muskrat, and two moose. Over the last six and a half years in the North Country, or two full weeks on earth (counting all the hours on earth Morgan and Eli were *not* on Askí, because time didn't stop for the animal beings when the children weren't there), the village had grown. Other beings had settled there, and where there used to be seven longhouses, there were now fourteen.

It was a jovial feast. The animal beings were genuinely happy for Morgan, who, along with Eli, had become a fixture in Misewa. Just as Muskwa had promised on their departure, after they had helped to save the village, the siblings were always welcome. When they returned to earth following their first visit, Morgan and Eli had come back the very next night, and they'd stayed for eight weeks on Askí. They'd returned every night, even on weekends, and stayed eight weeks each time. Tonight was the last night of their eighth week, and a fitting night for a feast. After eating, Morgan and Eli would return to earth through the Great Tree, and the beings in Misewa would see them again in about four months.

Morgan felt proud. It had taken her all this time to draw up the courage to hunt. She'd never been sure that she could take another living thing's life, but, over time, she had come to understand how important it was to the animal beings in Misewa, and to Indigenous people on earth, to hunt, trap, and fish for their subsistence. And if she were going to learn everything about traditional living, she needed to live a fully traditional life. That included hunting.

The circular field of bright, lush grass in front of the Council Hut was as full as the bellies of the villagers, and yet the celebration felt somehow empty. To the villagers, to Eli, and to Morgan. Because while six years had passed since the return of the Green Time, while there was Chief and Council, while the villagers gathered, both new and old . . . one was missing, and always would be.

Ochek.

The fire was large, and bright as a city streetlight; plumes of smoke billowed into the air, making it difficult to see the evening sky. And sitting with Eli and all the Misewa villagers, Morgan felt suddenly alone. She took deep breaths, trying to calm the sensation in her chest. Eli and Arik were busy picking food off each other's plates, Arik taking Eli's berries and bannock, and Eli taking Arik's meat. "I'm really more of a nut person anyway," she'd said. Every being seemed busy with another being, or their plates, and so Morgan slipped away from the food, the fire, the villagers, her brother, and the clearing. She needed to see Ochek . . . or the next best thing, his constellation in the sky.

As she walked away, she could hear her friend Emily's voice in her head. *You're seriously ghosting a feast in your honor?*

Back on earth, it had been incredibly hard for Morgan not to talk to anyone about this new world. She wasn't about to tell her foster parents, but Morgan wanted to tell somebody. The only person she could think of was Emily, because Emily was her only friend. But if she ever told

Emily, then she'd *have* to bring Emily to Askí. And who knew if Emily would tell anybody else? Next thing you knew, another person like Mason could come through the portal and ruin everything all over again. Keeping the secret was the hardest part of the last two weeks.

That, and missing Ochek.

Morgan wasn't sure if walking out into the darkness so that she could see the stars clearly would make the pain of losing Ochek any less intense. Staring up into the sky at Ochekatchakosuk, as Ochek had been renamed after dying, felt like staring at a photograph of somebody after you lost them. The kind of torture that only loss could bring. But Morgan didn't think she could stop, even if she wanted to. When she got far enough away from Misewa that the lights from the village couldn't reach her, she lay on her back, cradled her head in her hands, her fingers interlaced, and gazed at the constellation.

"Hey," she said. She spoke in a whisper at first, unsure that she was talking to anybody. But as she talked—more hopeful, as the moments passed, that she was—her words became more confident. "Are you really there?"

Yes, Iskwésis.

"Oh, now that we're in a long-distance friendship, you're back to calling me 'Girl,' are you?"

You haven't changed one bit, Morgan.

"Yeah," she said, "but you're a lot shinier than I remember. And you might've gained some weight. You're a little, like, boxy."

Must be all the stardust.

"You haven't lost your sense of humor, I guess."

I guess not.

The ground shook at Morgan's side like a tiny earthquake. She turned her head to find Muskwa had sat down, but they exchanged no greeting. They stayed like that, the bear sitting and Morgan lying down, for some time, quietly studying the same constellation.

After a bit, Morgan asked, "Do you think that's actually him?"

"I do," Muskwa said. "I think it's his spirit."

Morgan sighed. "He's really just a bunch of, like, hydrogen and helium, though, right? In the end."

"What does that mean, little one? Hydrogen and helium?"

"Oh, it's just science, or astronomy, or both. Science probably. That's what stars are made of, not spirits. Not really."

"Science," the bear repeated.

"Yeah. Clearly the worst subject ever." Morgan blindly ran her hand over the ground, picked up a rock, and threw it, listening to it as it skipped across the ground then settled a few yards away.

"Are you okay, Morgan?"

"No." Morgan tried to wipe a tear from her cheek with the sleeve of her shirt without the bear noticing. "It's just that I miss him, and he's never coming back, and I want to have more than just stars."

"He's not really gone, though, dear one," Muskwa said. "To live in the hearts of others is not to die."

"And he'll live on through stories and all that crap, I know." Now a burning feeling came, right where her heart was. She sat up as though jump-started. "That doesn't mean he's actually alive, Muskwa!"

"Everybody dies," Muskwa said in such a way that Morgan thought the animal being was trying to keep his booming voice quiet. Even in a whisper, it was powerful.

"Please don't say, 'But not every man really lives,' because that's from a movie on earth called *Braveheart* and it's cheesy," Morgan said.

"I was going to say that there's nothing anybody can do to stop it."

"Oh." Morgan shrugged. "Well, that's kind of morbid. I would've preferred a cheesy movie line, to be honest."

"I hope that when I die, it's while doing something as selfless and brave as Ochek."

The bear tried to pick up a stone from the ground. He tried a few times, but his paws were too big, the stones too small. He eventually just swiped at the ground and some rocks scuttled away.

Morgan chuckled. "Silly old bear," she said with an English accent.

"Why are you talking funny?"

"Never mind."

They were silent again until Morgan continued with something she'd thought of often, although she hadn't voiced it to anyone.

"You know what I've been thinking, Chief?"

"What's that?"

"I had the bag in my arms," she said, "the bag holding the summer birds, I mean. I think I carried it all the way up the mountain when we were being chased by Mason. And at any given time, I could've just . . . opened it. Just like that."

Morgan raised her arms high above her head, towards

the sky, picturing the summer birds flying away. As if she were back in that moment. As if she had actually done that very thing.

"From the other side of the mountain," Muskwa said, "where you were at that time, the birds might not have come to Misewa straightaway. They might have started their cycle somewhere else."

"The stupid bag was sealed shut by, like, twine or something like that," she said. "Just a piece of twine. All I had to do was cut it."

"We were on the brink, Morgan. All of us were so close to death. Maybe another day, maybe another week, and somebody else would've died. We couldn't afford to wait for the summer birds to bring the Green Time."

"And do you know what would've happened then?" she asked. She held up a hand with all her fingers and her thumb raised, then lowered them as she made each point. "Ochek wouldn't have had to climb the tree. Mason wouldn't have shot him with an arrow. Ochek wouldn't have been placed in the sky like he is now. And maybe Mahihkan wouldn't have died either." She had only her thumb raised now and used it to point at herself. She poked herself right in the middle of the chest. "And I wouldn't be left thinking about all this all the time!"

"You need to let go of those regrets. They'll eat you from the inside. Ochek, he had to do what he had to do. It couldn't have happened any other way. And do you know why, child?"

Muskwa leaned forward, so close to Morgan that she could feel his breath against her skin. Their eyes met.

"Why?" she said with a quivering bottom lip.

"Because that's the way it happened." He placed his paw against her cheek and wiped at a tear that had fallen. "We need to look forward, not backward."

Morgan got up and walked away from the bear, away from his paw against her cheek, and towards the northern woods. She kept walking until she'd breathed deeply several times, then turned back and stopped when she was close to Muskwa again.

"I would change a lot of things if I could, you know. It's not just Ochek. I would change little things, like I'd have brought a jacket through the Great Tree the first time I came here. Warmer mitts *for sure.*" She turned away, and looked down at the desolate surface at her feet. There, in the Barren Grounds. "And I would change bigger things. I'd tell my mom not to give me away."

"Easier said than done," Muskwa said.

"Easier said than done," Morgan said.

Morgan stood in front of the bear and eventually locked eyes with him. Then, he wrapped his enormous arms around her and she disappeared in his embrace. It felt like she'd buried herself in a comforter. She didn't think she ever wanted to leave, and she didn't, until they'd stayed like that long enough that the noise of the feast had died down. It felt like it was only them in the entire world.

In the quiet, with her voice muffled by Muskwa's fur, she asked, "Do you think it's boring up there in the sky?"

"I think it's peaceful."

Morgan swiveled around, keeping Muskwa's arms around her. There she observed the sky and all its stars, including the most important set of them.

The boxy body, the broken tail.

"Yeah, I guess you're right."

"I usually am, being the Chief and all. It goes with the job."

"Holy," Morgan said, "all of you think you're funny now, don't you?"

THREE

Eli was sitting in front of the fire, beside Arik, when Morgan walked into Ochek's old lodge, which was now the squirrel's. Arik hadn't done much to it in the time that she'd lived there. In fact, Morgan couldn't pick out even one significant change, except for a few pictures on the walls that Eli had drawn for Arik. Not ones that would open portals, just drawings of the village up close, a portrait of Arik, one of Ochek, and some of the earth: a city, Eli's home community, his grandfather's trapline. The papers were affixed to the walls with the only thing in the village that came from earth: thumbtacks. They covered some of the notches Ochek had made to count the days that Misewa had endured the White Time. To the uninformed, the notches might have seemed decorative, like stucco or something of the sort. But to Arik, Morgan, and Eli, they recounted history as vividly as the ocher paintings on the walls of the Council Hut. Each notch represented a day that no longer meant suffering, but resilience.

As soon as Morgan arrived, Eli and Arik abruptly stopped talking and looked guilty, as though they had been telling secrets. Morgan was pretty sure they had been, but she had learned, over the considerable time they'd spent together, that when Eli didn't want to share something with her, or anybody else, he would not. She had to wait until he was ready, and there was no forcing the matter. Morgan sat down across the fire from the pair, stuck her hands out to warm them, and just looked at them suspiciously. They deserved suspicion, at least.

She was given a hint of what their secret was when, after minutes of quiet, Eli asked, "Do you think we could stay a bit longer this time?"

Morgan shook her head. "Eli, you know we can't."

"Just a week? That's only one hour on earth."

This was the first time she'd ever heard Eli sound whiny. Wasn't that supposed to be a typical younger sibling thing? Like taking your favorite sweaters or books or whatever they could get their hands on? Was he going to start borrowing her clothing now?

Morgan shook her head more assertively this time. "You know the rules."

"We get back at, like, six in the morning. What's the difference if we get back at seven?"

"We've talked about this," Morgan said through her teeth. "If we leave at 10:00 at night and get back at 6:00 in the morning, Katie and James are dead asleep. If we left earlier or came back *later*, it's way more likely one of them would be up. And if one of them was up—"

"And they checked on us, we wouldn't be in bed," Eli said. "And then they'd check the attic room because—"

"They allow us up there," she said. "But we wouldn't be there. We wouldn't be anywhere *on earth*. And they're our foster parents, so they'd freak out, call the cops, and then, at some point, we would saunter out of the attic like rabbits out of a hat."

Eli's head dropped. "And they'd lock us out of the secret room for good."

"Goodbye, Misewa," she said.

"Wow," Arik said after a long silence, "you've really thought this through."

"Misewa Math sucks," Eli grumbled. "It's not like it's calculus or something. It's really just guessing, not for sure an answer, like one plus one is two. Misewa Math is saying one plus one is probably maybe around—"

"You want to keep coming here, don't you?" Morgan asked. "Misewa Math isn't just figuring out how many weeks we're here and how many hours it is on earth. It's figuring out when those hours have to be so that we can have more weeks here." Morgan stood up, walked around the fire, and sat down beside her brother. She put her arm around him. "So that we know when it's time to leave."

"Can we at least leave in the morning?"

Morgan thought about it. By then, if they slept eight hours, it'd be less than ten minutes on earth. What was ten minutes? "Yeah, we can leave in the morning, kid. Sure."

"Ekosani."

"You're welcome. But as soon as we're up, we've got to go. I know you want to come back. I know we both do."

Eli still refused to look up, but he nodded. Then he leaned to the side and rested his head against her shoulder. She placed her cheek against the top of his head and stared into the fire, watching the embers jump from the flames when the burning wood snapped or crackled. They looked like they were dancing in the air like stars. Like constellations. She watched them until they disappeared.

Arik cleared her throat.

"Yes, Arik?" Morgan said.

"First of all, let me just say that you two are really adorable," she said. "But I was wondering something, and I didn't want to interrupt or ruin the mood or something silly like that."

"*You* didn't want to ruin the mood?" Morgan said. "Since when?"

Even Eli, in his despondency, managed to chuckle.

"Yes, well," Arik said. "*Anyway.* I was wondering how a wapos would come out of a hat on earth. Do they stay in hats there? Not, say, in a burrow?"

"*Heeere* we go." Morgan smiled, and before they all went to bed she explained idioms to the squirrel. And when that didn't clear up the confusion, she explained magic tricks, too.

Morgan and Eli stayed in the bedroom of Arik's longhouse when they came to Misewa, sleeping in the same spots they had on their first journey. Arik was quite happy to sleep in the other room. The children had both tried to convince her to stay in her own bed but, truthfully, she wouldn't have it any other way. "Where would your guests sleep on earth?" she'd asked. "Plus, anything beats sleeping in a tree, children."

They had even established a bedtime routine. Arik would tuck Morgan and Eli in, pulling their hide comforters right up to their chins. And then, with Arik sitting by the fire, between their beds, one of them would tell a story. One night, Arik would recite a tale that belonged to Askí. The next night, Eli would describe a legend or a memory from his community. When it was Morgan's turn, she'd be less particular. It would be a shortened version of a book she'd read, or what she could remember of something she'd written herself. To Morgan, these felt inadequate, because she was telling tales of made-up fantasy in a world with real walking, talking animals, but it was all she could think of. Rarely did she describe something from her own childhood. Rarely did she want to, and she couldn't remember much anyway.

Tonight, it was Arik's turn, which made the siblings happy as they were enthralled by her stories. Yes, they'd been a part of a significant story themselves, one that had happened in Misewa, but there were so many others.

"Do you want to know why, long ago, there were no dogs on Askí?" she asked.

"Yes," Morgan and Eli said, one after the other.

"Let me tell you."

The stories always started in the same way. Arik would ask: Did the siblings want to learn about this thing or that thing? Yes, they did, without fail. Next, Arik would say,

"Let me tell you," before starting the story. Sometimes, the story would take a few minutes. Other times, it would take an hour. "In the good words," Arik had claimed once, "I could tell a story that would last days, and then you'd never get home in time!" Morgan and Eli didn't doubt her. Eli said that he'd heard the same thing about days-long stories from Elders in his community. It reminded Morgan of that old fantasy movie *The NeverEnding Story*. She tried to imagine sitting there for days listening to one tale, and couldn't. But she thought one day, if she learned Cree, she might try.

Arik's story began.

"It was a sad time when there were no dogs, naturally, because a lonely young one had no friend, and an Elder had no helper to fetch things for them. Many beings back then, long before the endless White Time, were nomadic. They had no four-legged creatures to assist with their marches, and no protection when danger was near." Arik howled like a dog to demonstrate the kind of protection she meant. A sort of alert, Morgan figured.

Arik went on. "Now, of course, because there weren't ever dogs, the beings didn't know they needed dogs; they just knew they needed *something*." Arik paused thoughtfully. "Now that I think about it, I'm not sure where Misewa's dogs went after dogs became a thing."

Morgan and Eli waited for her to recall, but they were met with silence until she shrugged.

"Maybe they saw a squirrel." She chuckled. "Seriously, though, Misewa had birds as protectors at one time, not dogs, and isn't that something? Birds!"

"Birds?" Eli said. "How would birds protect a village?"

"They weren't just any birds, but that's another story," Arik said. "For now, we're talking about dogs. My bad, though, because I did let my mind wander."

"This isn't really sounding much like a traditional story," Morgan teased.

"She just got sidetracked," Eli said confidently.

"*Anyhow.*" Arik was undeterred. "One day, a group of villagers, from right here in Misewa, set out to find help for their young ones, their Elders, and all the beings on Askí. They traveled far, to the Council of Wolves, and convened with them, expressing their concerns."

At the mention of wolves, Eli perked up. Hearing about wolves undoubtedly made Eli think of Mahihkan, whose death he continued to lament.

"It was decided that two wolf pups would be dispatched to each village on Askí, and so off they were sent, in all four directions. Over time, the pups grew, and adapted, and changed to become the first dogs on Askí."

"Is that actually true?" Morgan asked.

Arik sounded playful when she responded, "Some legends are history, some histories become legends."

"Oh, aren't you cute."

"Aren't I?"

"I used to have a dog," Eli said. "Used to. Like, a month and a half ago."

"In fairness," Morgan said, "it feels a lot longer than a month and a half—Misewa Math and all that."

"Tell me about this atim," Arik said.

Eli turned on his side. "His name was, *is*, Red. He's a mutt. Copper hair. Probably a shepherd and lab cross or something.

He has a tail that kind of curls up like a mosquito coil. It's so cute." He laughed, despite the sadness in his eyes.

"Is he, like, a rez dog?" Morgan asked. She'd heard about rez dogs from Eli. They were dogs who lived around the community, roaming free, hanging out at the grocery store entrance begging for food, playing with kids. She wasn't sure if rez dogs were owned by community members, but why wouldn't some be?

Eli shook his head. "He's my dog, but he never stays in the community. He lives on the trapline. He waits for me for when I go out with my moshom."

"Aww, that's sweet," Morgan said. "It's like that story—"

"Careful now," Arik said. "*Your* story time is another night."

"This one isn't days long." Morgan winked at the animal being. "Anyway, *Eli*, it's like that story about the dog who waited for its owner to come home every day, and then one day, the owner died, and the dog kept waiting and waiting . . ." As Morgan recapped the story, Eli looked progressively sadder, and finally she just trailed off. She realized she wasn't helping. "Never mind."

"Oh, now see," Arik said, "that story was far too short."

"It was just a summary of a story, and I didn't even finish it," Morgan said defensively. "Give me a break."

"Do you think he's still waiting for me?" Eli's eyes were glistening in the firelight.

"Yeah," Morgan said, "I think he is. Dogs are cool like that."

She wasn't sure if this was another thing she'd said wrong. Like, was it a good thing if Red was waiting for him? It was probably upsetting rather than comforting. Regardless, she *did* believe it, and one day, she decided right then, they would go on a different journey altogether, on their world. They would go to the land, just for her brother. They would find Red.

"I think that's enough storytelling for now," Arik said, "seeing as how this one"—she nodded towards Morgan—"hijacked my spotlight."

"It was, like, a ten-second story!" Morgan laughed.

"Good night, children." Arik performed the final part of their routine, which was to tuck them in all over again. She visited one sibling after the other, repositioning the comforters rather than pulling them up higher, kissed each of them on their forehead, then took her leave. "Until tomorrow."

"Until tomorrow," Morgan and Eli said in unison.

Morgan instantly settled in for a nice, long sleep, happy that they'd return to earth in the morning well-rested, and not worrying so much that they'd return to earth just before 6:10 a.m. rather than 6:00 a.m. She lay on her side, tucked her knees into her chest, and rested her head on some fur. She could not have been more comfortable. She closed her eyes and waited to fall asleep.

But sleep did not come.

When simply being cozy didn't help, she tried all sorts of things. Deep breathing. Clearing her mind. Even counting up to a hundred, twice. None of it worked. Frustrated, she opened her eyes with an intention to do some stretching before trying to sleep again. Instead, she found Eli with his eyes wide open, looking into the fire unblinking.

Morgan didn't let on that she was awake at first. She just watched him. He didn't notice her. He continued to look into the flames as though they were telling a story, as if the snapping and crackling of the wood was a language that only he could understand.

It was hard to read what was on his mind. He wasn't easy to read at the best of times, and now it felt impossible. His eyebrows were collapsed inward; his eyes looked wet and larger than normal; his lips were pursed. Morgan's best guess was that he was worried, or scared, or maybe both. She watched him for as long as she could before it became too much to just look at him and not do anything. It felt like passing an accident scene and not stopping to help. At last she pushed her heavy comforter to the side, got up from her bed, walked around the fire, and lay down behind her brother. She wrapped her arm around him.

Eli didn't look at her. He didn't move at all, other than to clasp her forearm. That said more than any words, but Morgan was left to decipher it.

"Hey," she said lightly, "you okay?"

He breathed deeply, the way she did when she felt angry, but only once. "I don't want to leave."

Morgan mimicked his breath in a prolonged sigh. "I feel like we've had this conversation before." She propped herself up for a moment to try to make eye contact with him, but when she couldn't, she settled back down behind him. "I don't like leaving either, but it's just a day, and then we'll be here for *weeks.* You know that."

"A day is too long."

"Eli," she whispered, "a day is a day. Tomorrow will come before you know it, and we'll be back. Promise."

He didn't respond for so long that Morgan thought he might be sleeping, long enough that her eyelids became heavy. But then he repeated what he'd said, only this time he sounded desperate.

"A day is too long."

That was the last thing either of them said. They lay there awake, Eli staring at the fire, Morgan staring at Eli. At some point, when the fire was almost out and the light was low against the walls, he began to snore. But Morgan was far too worried about him to sleep now. She'd never seen him like this. He had been quiet, but not this sort of quiet. He had been sad, but not this sort of sad. He had longed for home on earth, but now he was longing for this world to be his home and saying that the hours on earth were somehow going to pass as slowly as they did on Misewa.

But they weren't. She knew it, and so did he. What was so bad, then, about waiting a day?

All of these thoughts kept her awake, and when morning came, Morgan couldn't remember falling asleep at all. She'd been happy to stay overnight, to get some rest before returning to earth, and then she'd not slept. Staying over had been completely useless.

By the time Morgan and Eli crawled through the portal and set foot in their secret room at 6:09 a.m., she was more tired than she would have been if she'd insisted they leave the night before. She was more tired, Eli was sad, and it felt as though all they could do was wait for things to get better.

Wait fifteen hours and fifty-one minutes, to be exact.

FOUR

Morgan crawled into her own bed, intending to stay there for as long as humanly possible. Even though she was still worried about Eli, who had been just as sad that morning when they left, she was exhausted from her sleepless night. She curled up under her comforter, buried her head in her pillow, closed her eyes, and was dead to the world in seconds. She couldn't have stayed awake even if she'd wanted to.

It was a dreamless one-hour sleep that seemed to pass in a heartbeat. Morgan's alarm jolted her awake at 7:00 a.m. She got dressed quickly, throwing on ripped jeans, a white shirt, and a hoodie. Her moccasins, which she had become attached to, completed her outfit.

Walking across the hallway, she entered Eli's bedroom. He was a mound under his *Star Wars* comforter, unmoving except for the gentle rise and fall of his breathing. She was envious that he was still sleeping, but concerned because he was usually awake when she got up, often downstairs at the dining room table with his breakfast already in front of him. She found the shape of his shoulder underneath the comforter and nudged him. He moaned and turned away from her. She sat on the bed and pulled the comforter down, exposing his head.

"Hey," she said, "it's time to get up."

Strands of black hair from Eli's head, escaping from his braid, were like lonely blades of sweetgrass in the southern woods. Morgan knew that the braid was sacred, just as the sweetgrass they picked at the banks of the river on Askí was sacred. The way he braided it meant something to him—it was a source of strength. She could see his hair, the side of his face, and one eyelid fluttering open. She took that as a cue to nudge him again.

"Come on. I can smell breakfast."

Morgan breathed in to catch the aroma. The food in Misewa was amazing, but there were things they didn't have that she missed after weeks away there. Things that weren't as healthy, but were just as delicious. And she'd come to like the smell of coffee, even though James didn't like her drinking it.

"Isn't she too young?" James had asked Katie more than once when Morgan poured herself a cup at the breakfast table.

"Kids her age drink coffee," Katie had assured him. "They drink iced coffees like we used to have Slurpees."

Eli didn't move after Morgan's urging. He just lay there, turned away from her, eyes open, staring out the window.

"We're going to be late," she said. "And then James or Katie will have to drive us. Do you know how embarrassing it is to get dropped off by your parents?"

"I'm not going," Eli said without looking at her.

"What do you mean you're not going?" Morgan got up from Eli's bed, walked around the foot of it, and sat on the other side, so he had to at least face her if he wasn't going to look at her. She tried to guess what he was thinking by assessing his facial expression, just as she had the night before.

"I said I'm not going."

Eli didn't even try to turn away. If he missed Misewa so much, lying in bed all day wouldn't get him there any faster. The days on earth already passed slowly when they went to school, and even more slowly on the weekends.

"Why?" she asked.

"I don't feel good," he said.

"You're not sick. You're not coughing or anything." She reached forward and felt his forehead like a mother would. It was dry, and a normal temperature. Then it hit Morgan like a gust of blizzard wind.

"You're playing hooky!" she said with a gasp.

"I am not," he said defensively.

"You're going to go without me." She stood up and started pacing back and forth while going over the plan she was sure he'd concocted. "Katie and James will be at work. They don't get home until, like, five. Let's say, just to be safe, they'll be home at the earliest at four. That means you'll have . . . eight weeks in Misewa." She stopped and crouched in front of Eli so that he could do nothing but look at her unless he closed his eyes. He didn't, though. He looked right at her. "Eight weeks! Fifty-six days! That's two months! That's how long we stay when we go together!"

"I'm not going to go to Misewa!" Eli burst into a sitting position. "I wouldn't go there without you."

"You went without me the first time," Morgan said. "And you didn't want to leave Askí last night. Why else would you stay home from school and fake sick?"

"Well, I wouldn't go without you *now*," Eli said. "You should know that."

"I thought I did, but I don't know what else could be going on with you. Can't you just tell me? Haven't we been through enough? I'm your sister." She moved a bit closer to him, shuffling along the side of the bed. "Right, *brother*?"

"Yeah."

"Okay, so . . ." She reached forward and put her hand on his forearm. She pulled at it gently to uncross his arms. "Tell me. I know you don't like sharing feelings, but *just this once* . . ."

Eli looked close to tears, and he had that face again, full of sadness and worry. It was a look that, last night, was unfamiliar, but now Morgan was accustomed to it.

"It's not that I want to sneak off to Misewa," he said, "even though I'd like to just live there all the time."

"Then what?" she asked, her hand still on his forearm.

He started to cry. "I don't want to go to school."

"Why don't you want to go to school?"

"I told you before that you don't need to know every single thing, and I *don't* have to share my feelings."

"And I told you that I do, in fact, need to know every single thing." Morgan laughed softly, but Eli just lay there. So she sat. A minute later, she thought that he had gone back to sleep, and she watched as the comforter rose, then fell.

At least he was still breathing.

“You guys!” Katie called from the first floor, sounding slightly annoyed. Morgan could tell because, even through the closed door that opened to the stairs, her voice was clear. “It’s late, and your breakfast is getting cold!”

“Hey!” Morgan said with mock excitement. “I could make your food into a happy face if that’d help! What do you think?” She did her best James impression: “*You’ve seemed so sad lately.*”

Eli grunted loudly, then kicked off his comforter. “Alright, I’m up! Get out so I can get dressed.”

Morgan, feeling pleased with herself, left Eli’s bedroom.

“See you downstairs,” she said while crossing the hall to the stairs. Then she added, in a melodic tone, “And this isn’t over.”

“Yes, it is,” Eli said. “And don’t touch my food!” he warned before Morgan shut the door to the second floor.

It was weird to be the one waiting for Eli at the dining room table. Morgan’s breakfast was in front of her, a delicious-looking plate of scrambled eggs, sausages, hash browns, and toast. There was even cheddar cheese shredded and sprinkled atop the eggs. The food was accompanied by a glass of orange juice. She drank that while waiting, then poured herself a cup of coffee. Black. James and Katie shared the same exchange they always did about Morgan drinking coffee.

Soon after, Eli joined them, and without so much as a greeting, he sat down at his place. It was one word less than what Morgan had offered when she’d come to sit at the table. She’d slid out a chair, plunked down as though she’d been carrying a fifty-pound sack, and said, “Morning.”

"Why do you both look like zombies?" James asked.

"Tired." Morgan knew her foster parents didn't like one-word responses, but she couldn't muster up more than that.

"You guys didn't stay up late hanging out in that attic room again, did you?" Katie asked. "You know it's not really safe up there while it's being renovated."

"It's *always* going to be in the middle of the renovation," Morgan said.

"We've let you up there once or twice, but what if one of you steps on a nail and gets . . ." Katie paused thoughtfully for a word, but finally turned to James for help. "What do you get when you step on a nail?"

"Hurt?" James said.

"*James*, contribute, okay?"

"Maybe if you hired new guys, the attic would get finished and we could go up there all the time and you wouldn't have to worry about us getting *tetanus*," Morgan said.

"Oh yeah, that's it," James said, then held his arms out as though he had a gun pointed at him. "Heart guy, sorry."

The fact that they were allowed to go up to their secret room at all was probably their foster parents' way of acknowledging that they were both old enough to need a private place of their own. Now, according to James, they looked like the undead, and Morgan worried that their privileges might get cut off. She shot Eli a look, like, *get it together*, and he nodded unconvincingly.

"We weren't even up there." Morgan tried to sound chipper. "We were reading. Well, *I* was reading. Eli was drawing. In my room. Not the attic."

"Yeah." Eli attempted to perk up.

"I think a walk will help us wake up, actually." Morgan wanted to end this conversation. "Hey, Eli? We should go."

"Yeah." Eli put his fork down and got up from the table with the sort of energy he'd lacked the entire morning and the night before.

"If we don't leave now, we'll be late." Morgan got up too. It would be a much-needed brisk walk on a cool autumn morning. Better than a cup of coffee.

"Could you catch up to Eli?" James asked Morgan. "Katie and I wanted to . . ." His words trailed off. He looked nervous, as though he didn't want to risk a classic Morgan blowup.

"We have something for you," Katie said, standing up..

James took the cue and stood beside her. Morgan backed away.

"*Not* moccasins or anything like that," James said. "We've learned our lesson. *Lessons.*"

"Although it looks like you might need a new pair." Katie glanced at Morgan's black moccasins. They were only two weeks old in earth time, but of course they looked much older.

Morgan stepped forward to get them out of Katie's view and did her best to change the subject.

"What did you want to talk to me about?" she asked hurriedly.

"I'll walk slow so you can catch up," Eli said, taking the hint.

"You walk slow anyway," Morgan pointed out.

Katie, James, and Morgan stayed where they were, standing around the dining room table, while Eli got his things at the front door. Morgan could hear him slip his fall jacket on, take his backpack off the hook, slide his shoes on, and secure his drawing pad underneath his arm.

The front door opened; the front door closed.

"So, what's up?" Morgan asked.

Neither Katie nor James answered. They just looked at each other like kids waiting to see who was braver.

"I'm not going to freak out," Morgan promised. "I just"—she checked the time on her cellphone—"I've got to go. I don't want Eli to walk alone. *You* don't want Eli to walk alone. He's still getting used to . . . everything."

Katie reached across the dining room table, past the almost untouched breakfasts, and offered a folded Post-it Note to Morgan. Morgan looked at James and Katie with equal amounts of worry and curiosity before taking the note. She slipped it into her pocket.

"What is it?"

She did not want to look at it. She was fearful of that. Whatever Katie told her would determine whether she would ever take it out of her pocket. If it was something she didn't like, she'd leave it in her pants until they got washed and the note got ruined.

"It's, um . . ." Katie licked her trembling lips. "It's your mother's name and phone number. I got it from . . . well, that doesn't matter . . . I just got it. I thought you might want it, just in case."

"You . . ." Morgan felt the note through the fabric of her jeans with suddenly cold and sweaty fingertips. "You thought I might . . . want it . . . because . . ."

Morgan's heart began to jackhammer. She felt as though her hoodie was vibrating for everyone to see. *Thump, thump,*

thump, thump, thump, thump, thump. But her chest wasn't burning. She did not feel anger. She didn't know what she felt. She took several deep breaths that did not help whatsoever.

Then she whispered, "*Kiskisitotaso,*" without thinking about it.

"What was that?" Katie asked.

"Nothing," Morgan said. "I didn't say anything."

"Listen, you don't have to call or anything; we just thought that you might want to . . . one day," James explained.

"I have to go," Morgan said. "I have to go *now.* Eli will be . . ."

But she didn't finish her sentence. She backed away from the table, putting her worn-out moccasins in full view of her foster parents. Then she ran outside, taking nothing with her except the Post-it Note, still in her pocket.

FIVE

On the way to school, all Morgan could do was think about the dream she'd been having of her mother, the dream that she thought was a memory. There was her mother, rocking her, Morgan, as a toddler. There was her mother, humming a song to keep her calm. There was her mother, saying that word to her in Cree. "Kiskisitotaso." *Don't forget about who you are.* There was Morgan being taken away by two strangers, her mother being held back.

Morgan heard her mother's voice as clear as she saw the dream. She heard her mother's voice as she walked Eli to his locker, the word even taking her attention away from his mysterious worry. She heard her mother's voice rise above the thunderous noise of students, shoulder to shoulder in the hallways like rush hour traffic. And she heard her mother's voice now, standing in front of her opened locker, staring into it blankly. She had her hand pressed against her thigh, over the pocket of her jeans, and she could feel the outline of the Post-it Note Katie had written her mother's name and number on.

But she didn't take it out to look at it.

So many questions swirled around in her thoughts, the chief one being: What would she say first if she called? *Hi, Mom.* No. *Hi, whatever your name is, how are you doing? Where've you been? Why'd you let me go?* That was a good way to get hung up on, not so much start a conversation. *Hey, it's Morgan. Remember me?* That felt like a guilt trip, so a definite no.

Morgan closed her locker without taking anything out, but still stood there, holding the lock in her hand, staring at the door. She didn't know Emily was right there until her friend cleared her throat.

"What's going on with you, Morg?"

"Huh?"

"Oh, are we not doing nicknames anymore? Because I've been 'Houldsy' and you've been 'Morg' and I've really liked it."

"I . . ."

"You're kind of reminding me of a zombie right now," Emily said. "I mean, you've been distant the last week or so, but this is on another level."

"My foster parents share your opinion," Morgan said. "Sorry, it's just been the worst morning. And confusing, and—"

"Hey." Emily gave Morgan a hug just as Morgan was certain that tears were about to flood out of her eyes. Emily must have seen them welling up. "It's alright."

"I just don't know what to do," Morgan sobbed into Emily's sweatshirt. She pressed her face into the fabric so that nobody could see her crying, even though everybody would know that she was. She could feel her entire body moving in rhythm with her stuttered breaths.

"About what?" Emily had rested her chin on Morgan's shoulder and wrapped her arms around Morgan's waist.

"About anything!"

"I mean," Emily whispered, "can you elaborate a bit?"

The bell rang. It jolted Morgan, and Emily squeezed her tighter, as though, if she didn't, Morgan might float away. Morgan hadn't noticed the crowd in the hallway thin out but now she heard footsteps racing towards classes—the sound of sneakers squeaking against waxed floors.

"How about we skip English?" Emily said.

"And go where?" Morgan asked.

"Come with me."

Morgan followed Emily away from their lockers and the classroom, down the hallway, and into the bathroom. The brick walls were painted a washed-out orange, as though they'd been sun-bleached. The floor was speckled with gray and black and brown and looked like marble but probably wasn't. The bathroom stalls were puke green. But even though it was kind of ugly and not really comfortable, it was private, especially with everyone else in class.

Morgan and Emily sat on the floor at the far end of the bathroom, at the end of the line of bathroom stalls, underneath the large frosted window, with their backs against the gross orange wall. For the first few minutes after class had started, they just sat and listened and watched the door. Morgan expected to see Mrs. Edwards storm into the bathroom and drag them by their ears into class. They'd get detention. They'd have to write a poem about their behavior. But the minutes passed, and Mrs. Edwards did not come.

"So . . . ," Emily said, once the coast was obviously clear.

Morgan played dumb. "So . . . what?"

"You said that you didn't know what to do. I asked you about what, and you said about anything. *So . . . ?*"

Morgan tightened her lips in a straight, unbreakable line. Where could she start? "I guess, first of all, there's something wrong with Eli."

"How so?"

"Like, he's always been quiet, but last night and this morning, he just seems sad. Or worried. I can't tell. Just . . ."

"Something's not right."

"Yeah, and I don't know what to do. I feel like his big sister, and—"

"That's a change from calling him the kid you live with two weeks ago," Emily broke in.

Morgan ignored the interruption and continued. "A big sister is supposed to be able to help her little brother, and I can't, or he won't let me, because I ask him what's wrong and he won't tell me. How do I get him to tell me?"

"Obviously, I'm not the one to give advice," Emily said. "I've been wondering how to get *you* to open up to *me*. I thought you were going to tell me why you've been so weird lately."

Morgan closed her eyes and buried her face in her hands. "I'm sorry. I've had a lot on my mind."

"Seems like it. You've been pretty distant, but today it's not the same kind of distant."

"That's what's second of all," Morgan said. "I had this, kind of, fight with my foster parents a while ago, and the subject of my mom came up. Like, my birth mom. And Katie, my *foster* mom, she went and found my birth mom's name and phone number."

"Are you serious?" Emily asked. "Is that bad?"

Morgan dug her hand into her pocket and pulled out the Post-it Note. She held it up, pinched between her index finger and thumb. "I haven't looked at it yet. That's why I said I didn't know what to do. Not about Eli and not about this."

"Okay, okay, okay," Emily said, slowly and softly. "Let's work this out."

"How?" Morgan wanted to hear Emily's ideas, because she didn't have any herself.

"Okay, well . . . first of all, Eli will tell you when he's ready to tell you," Emily said. "You can't push him. I mean, boys don't really open up anyway, so you're just going to have to be patient."

"I kind of know that about him," she admitted. "He's not really a sharer." She groaned in frustration. "Are you saying *all* boys are like that?"

"I have a brother, okay? And yes, boys are, like . . . emotionally . . . dumb. Or stunted or something. They don't like to talk about stuff unless it's video games or sports."

"*You* like to talk about sports."

"Yeah, and feelings not so much." Emily leaned closer as if there was somebody else in the bathroom and she was about to reveal the world's biggest secret. "That's why I know about boys. I can get in their heads."

"And you're calling *me* weird."

"And about *that*." Emily pointed to the Post-it Note. "Answer fast without thinking. Do you want to talk to your mom?"

Morgan paused. She did want to talk to her mom. She had talked to her mom in her dreams. She and her dream mom had really connected. They'd connected so well, and the connection had seemed so real, that Morgan, at the same time, *didn't* want to talk to her mom. Because maybe, just maybe, she was wrong and her mom hadn't wanted her. She *thought* she'd dreamed a memory, but what if she hadn't? What if it was just a dream? What if her mother had just . . . let her go?

"I . . ."

"I told you not to think, Morg."

"I guess I—"

Before Morgan could finish, the bathroom door started to open. The movement announced itself with a creak. Morgan and Emily shared a look of panic. They'd been caught. They scrambled into the last bathroom stall to hide.

The bathroom door shut. Footsteps moved from the door towards the sinks. While the mystery person stalked across the floor, Emily and Morgan climbed up onto the toilet without making a sound, each of them with an index finger pressed against her lips.

The footsteps stopped.

Morgan and Emily stared at each other wide-eyed. Emily motioned towards the bathroom stall door. Morgan thought this was her asking who it was. Morgan shrugged. Emily pointed up. Morgan interpreted this too: Emily wanted her to look. Morgan mouthed, "No!" to Emily. Emily mouthed, "Yes!" to Morgan. They continued their silent argument until finally Morgan relented. She straightened up, and stood as tall as she could to peer over the bathroom stall. When she saw who it was, she gasped, then jumped off the toilet and burst out of the stall with Emily right behind her.

And there they stood, face-to-face with Eli.

SIX

"Eli!" Morgan shouted.

"Dude, you can't be in the girls' bathroom." Emily had her arms crossed and looked generally unimpressed.

"What are you doing in here?" Morgan asked.

Eli looked stunned. There were several agonizing seconds of silence. In those seconds, Morgan noticed that his face was flushed, he looked more distressed than worried, and for some reason he had a pair of scissors clutched in his hand.

"Nothing," he muttered.

Morgan and Emily exchanged an unconvinced look. Then Morgan turned back to Eli. "It's not nothing. You're a bad liar."

Eli kept glancing at Emily, and Morgan realized that he didn't want to say anything with her there. She couldn't blame him. He didn't know Emily. Morgan took Emily's hand and led her over to the bathroom door. They huddled there while Eli turned away from them, back towards the sink.

He leaned forward and grabbed the sides of the sink as though he needed it for support, the scissors pressed between his palm and the porcelain.

"Would you think I'm a total jerk if I asked you to give us a few minutes?" Morgan asked.

Emily nodded, but it was hard to tell if she was really cool with it or if her feelings were hurt. Morgan felt a pang of fear. They'd only really been hanging out for two weeks, and apparently Morgan had been distant and weird. Emily was popular. She didn't need Morgan. At least, Morgan didn't think so. She still wasn't sure why Emily had decided to befriend her at all. But Emily squeezed Morgan's hand.

"I'll hang around in the hallway and try not to get caught."

"Really?"

"Yeah, really."

They gave each other a quick hug, then Emily left.

Eli was still leaning against the sink. Morgan hesitated, then approached her brother. She leaned against the sink beside Eli's, facing the bathroom stalls.

It was quiet.

Morgan asked the same question she had earlier. "What are you doing here? I know it's not an accident."

Eli just shook his head.

"Come on, kid," she said. "You can't just stand there and say nothing."

"I don't like it when you call me kid," he said.

"Okay. I won't call you kid. I'm sorry."

Morgan watched Eli's face carefully as he stared down at the sink. A tear dropped from his eye and landed perfectly in the center of the drain, as if he'd aimed it that way. Before long, another tear fell. This one landed against the porcelain and slid into the drain.

"What's wrong?" Morgan wanted to cry just seeing him like this. He was worse now than the night before or this morning. Whatever he'd been feeling was building up inside of him, and she felt that he was about to explode. "Please."

He looked at her. His eyes were desperately sad. He picked his braid off his shoulder. "Girls in my class have been pulling my braid."

"Like, *pulling* it pulling it? Like, hard? Or just tugging at it?"

"Does it matter?"

"Well, they might just like you," she said, "but that doesn't make it okay."

"One of them said that she wished she had my hair, but she was saying it to somebody else and I just overheard it," he said. "Then they started laughing."

Morgan sighed. "Girls can be mean."

Eli wouldn't let go of his braid, like he wanted to pull it too. Pull it off maybe. That's how hard he was grasping it. His hand was shaking.

"Why would that make you come in here, though?"

"Because." His tears really started to fall. His voice began to shake, like his hand, so much that it was hard to understand him. Talking through tears was the hardest thing. "Because there are guys in my class who don't let me go to the boys' bathroom."

"They don't let you *what*?" Morgan asked loud enough that a teacher could have heard her from the hallway, but she wasn't thinking about teachers or detention.

"They block me from going to the bathroom." Eli looked towards the door as though the guys were there now. "They stand there and make me go in here. They say"—he had to catch his breath he was crying so hard, his chest heaving so violently—"they say, 'No girls allowed,' and make me go in here."

"Why do you listen to them?" Morgan asked. "Forget them. Emily and I will bring you in there right now. Let's go. You can go."

"They'll beat me up if they catch me in there. They said they would. That's why I don't try anymore, even when they're not around. Even during class."

"Have you seen Emily's legs? She plays hockey. One kick and they'd be dead."

"It's not funny." Eli turned away. Back to staring at the drain, his braid still in his hand.

"I didn't think it was. I was just trying to . . ." Morgan sighed deeply "I'm sorry. I'm trying to be a good sister and I don't know what to say."

"There's nothing you *can* say."

"Is that why you wanted to stay in Misewa? Because you didn't want to deal with those stupid girls and those jerk guys?"

"Yes."

"Well," Morgan began to reason, "look. Soon it'll be nighttime, we'll be back there, and to us it'll be two months before you see those guys again. We'll, I don't know, learn some karate moves and beat them up if they bug you again."

"Beating up bullies is just being a bully too."

"Okay, fine, but there has to be something we can do so

they don't bug you again." She searched for a solution, but couldn't think of one. In the end, she offered, "We could go earlier, stay a *bit* longer earth time, and be there for way longer Misewa time. How about that?"

"That won't stop them. They've been doing it since I started coming to school here, and they'll do it no matter when I come back. It'll just be one day for them. And it'll be worse tomorrow. It's always worse."

"Why didn't you say anything?" Morgan asked. "I could've . . . I don't know . . . like, we've been close for so long now. You can't keep these things inside like that."

"I'm embarrassed," Eli said. "I'm crying like . . . like . . . like a *girl*. Just like they say I am."

"Everybody cries," she said. "Don't think crying makes you weak. It's totally cool. And they're *not* cool."

"I try to hide my braid in my sweater or under my shirt, and it doesn't matter because they know it's still there, and so do I. They just yank it out and keep calling me a girl anyway."

"So what? You're just going to take it? Keep waiting to go back to Misewa and wanting to stay when it's time to leave?"

Eli didn't say anything and he didn't shake his head. He just stood there, leaning against the sink, staring into the drain, holding his braid. "There's only one thing I can do." Eli pulled his braid out straight and started cutting through it with the scissors.

"No! Eli!"

Morgan lunged forward to stop him, but he turned away from her and kept cutting. She froze and could only watch as the scissors sliced through his hair and the braid fell to the ground.

SEVEN

Eli fell to his knees before the braided lock of hair, the long section of black strands still perfectly tied the way he always kept it. He wasn't crying anymore. His cheeks were wet and his eyes were red, but he just had a look of disbelief now, as though he couldn't understand what had just happened, what he'd just done.

Morgan sat beside him. She reached down and picked up the braid. It fell apart in her hands and spread over her palms like pooling water. The only thing keeping it together was the dark brown hair tie at one end.

"Ummm," Emily said from the door, "is everything okay in here?"

There was an awkward pause. Morgan and Eli didn't look away from the hair. She heard Emily walk closer to them, until she was standing over them. Then she heard Emily gasp.

"Oh my god, what happened? Your hair!"

Eli self-consciously pulled his hood up to cover his head.

"Some kids were teasing him about his braid," Morgan said.

"Teasing how?" Emily said, appalled.

"Just"—Morgan shook her head—"being jerks."

Emily crouched between Morgan and Eli. "I think your hair was . . . *is* . . . awesome. Don't ever listen to jerks."

Morgan could almost feel each strand of hair against her skin, as if it were alive. She started to braid it back the way it had been.

"It's too late now anyway," Eli said.

"Hey," Emily said. "Hair grows back. You just have to give it time, that's all."

Morgan, busily re-braiding the hair, nodded. "And your hair grows *super* fast, Eli." She was sure that he'd understand what she meant. Tonight they'd go to Misewa and they'd be there for weeks. Tomorrow, in earth time, his hair would be much longer. The only problem was how they'd explain the abnormal growth to Emily. He might just have to wear a hat for a while.

"They'll just start teasing me again," Eli said.

"They're bullies," Emily said flatly. "They'll just find something else to mess with you about anyway. It's not the hair, it's not you; it's them."

"If I could stop being brown, I'd do that too."

"Eli." Morgan said. "Don't say that. You don't mean that."

"What if I do? If kids are going to treat me this way because—"

"You've always been proud of being Cree, and you've helped me to be proud of it too. I never wanted to be Cree, didn't even know what Cree meant, until you came into my life."

Eli interlocked his fingers on top of his head, keeping the hood firmly in place, as though Morgan or Emily meant to pull it down. Or maybe he was trying to disappear.

"Your skin is perfect," Emily said. "People would kill for it, and nobody should change for anybody. Sometimes I think I should be doing 'girly' stuff but, like, what's 'girly' anyway?"

"Then what do I do?" Eli asked.

"You stick up for yourself," Emily said. "Don't let them talk to you like they do."

"And don't let them make you go to the girls' bathroom," Morgan added.

"They'll beat me up," Eli said.

Morgan finished the braid and tied an elastic on the other end. She hadn't done as good a job as Eli, but still, she was impressed. It was tight and clean. There weren't too many wayward strands. It looked like a braid of sweetgrass, but it didn't smell sweet. It smelled like bear grease. That's what he used to keep his hair shiny and slick while they were in Misewa. They hadn't had a chance to shower yet, since returning to earth. They were as clean as a nearby stream in the North Country could make them.

She handed the braided hair to Eli. He held it in his hands as if it were fragile, as though it might break if he was rough with it.

"What did you tell me about your braid?" Morgan asked, even though she knew the answer. She wanted Eli to remember it.

He curled his fingers around the hair. "It gives me pride in who I am."

"That's right. Don't ever lose that pride," she said. "And, like, you know how your braid is three sections that you weave together?"

"Yeah," Eli said. He seemed to know what she was going to say next.

"When they're apart, they're soft and flimsy. All the hair can fall apart easily. But when you put those three parts together . . ."

"It's stronger."

"Hey." Emily counted each one of them with her index finger, including herself. "There's three of us! What do you know?"

"We'll keep each other strong," Morgan said.

Eli looked up and managed a smile. He slid the braided hair into the kangaroo pocket of his sweatshirt. He made eye contact with Emily, then Morgan. There was regret in his eyes, but maybe, just maybe, a little less of what she'd seen in his face that morning and the night before.

"Thanks," he said again.

Class ended. The three of them got to their feet, not wanting to get caught sitting on the bathroom floor when other kids walked in, which they were bound to do. At break, the bathroom became a hangout, not a hideout.

With everything that had just happened with Eli, time

had gone by quickly, and Morgan didn't feel ready to be in the next class either. She didn't care that Katie and James would get an email notification that she'd not gone to class. She'd deal with that after school. And her foster parents wouldn't get after her too badly anyway.

Eli, she noticed, had one hand in the kangaroo pocket of his hoodie, no doubt holding the braided hair. She became aware that she had her hand on something too. She was unfolding and refolding the Post-it Note. Anxiously, confusedly, fearfully. So many emotions over one little piece of paper. The way that she and Eli had described braided hair, that's how she wanted to feel. Strong enough to make a simple phone call.

Emily walked to the door before the rush came in like a stampede. Eli went with her. Morgan stayed where she was.

"You coming?" Emily asked.

"I'll catch up," Morgan said. "Now I actually have to go to the bathroom."

"TMI, Morg." Emily winked at her, something a grandpa might do, which made Morgan smile, despite all the feelings taking up space in her brain. "I'll see you soon."

"Yeah," Morgan said. Then she locked eyes with Eli. "You okay?"

He nodded.

"Don't worry." Emily put her arm around his shoulders. "I'll get this guy to class first."

As kids filtered into the bathroom, Morgan ducked into a bathroom stall, locked it, and sat down on the closed toilet seat. She pulled the Post-it Note out of her pocket, unfolded it slowly and carefully as though she were doing origami in reverse, then stared at the name and the phone number. Her mother's name. She seemed suddenly real. Before, her mother had been nothing but an image. A dream of a memory. Now, she was Jenny Trout. Trout, like a fish. Morgan chuckled quietly at that.

Her mother's last name had caught her attention first, but soon all she could do was read the phone number over and over, as though she were memorizing it for a test. She took out her cellphone and added Jenny Trout to her contacts. The bell rang as she stared at her phone, and now that she was alone again, Morgan imagined her mom's name coming up as a photo—a photo of Morgan and Jenny, which Morgan would have taken after going to visit her, wherever she lived.

Morgan dialed the number. Her thumb hovered over the green button with the white telephone icon on it. She was so close to pressing down. Her thumb remained a millimeter away from the button long enough that it began to tremble. Then, with a tear slipping down her cheek, her thumb moved to the right and she pressed the delete button.

One by one, the numbers disappeared from the call screen.

Morgan still didn't know what she was going to say. *Hey, Mom. Can I call you Mom? That's cool. Hey, Jenny. I know it's been, what, a decade or something, but who's counting? Anyway, how's it going? It's me, your daughter. Morgan. Kiskisitotaso and all that.*

"That's so lame," she said to herself. "You're so lame."

Morgan pressed the screen lock and pushed the phone into her pocket. Maybe she could write a script or something, just so she'd have things to say that weren't stupid.

She could pretend that it was a writing project assigned by Mrs. Edwards: *What would you say to your long-lost mother?* But who knew if Jenny Trout even wanted Morgan to call her? Why would she want to talk to a kid she hadn't seen or heard from for ten years? Who had Katie even got Jenny's number from? From Jenny herself? Or from Child and Family Services? Probably CFS.

No way. Forget the script. Forget calling. Their conversations could be in Morgan's dreams, in her imagination. They couldn't get any better than that, so what was the point in trying?

EIGHT

After Morgan had pushed through the rest of her classes, after the bell had rung to signal the end of the school day, after she'd said goodbye to Emily and given her a drawn-out hug for all the help she'd been, Morgan found Eli waiting for her on the front steps of the school. His hood was up, his drawing pad tucked under his arm, and he was sitting hunched over and head down. It looked as though he thought he could hide in plain sight.

She walked up beside him and put a hand on his shoulder gently, so as not to startle him. That's when she saw that he'd been looking at the braided hair he'd cut off. He quickly returned it to his kangaroo pocket.

"Ready to go?" Morgan had almost added "kid" but remembered Eli's request to not call him that. Anything she could do to avoid upsetting him further was important.

"Ready." He got up as an old man might.

They walked down the steps together and joined the crowd of kids heading away from school. She fought for space on the front walk.

"What were you drawing today at lunch?" Morgan recalled how furiously Eli had been working in the gym that doubled as their cafeteria. He'd looked like a conductor during a particularly fast movement of a symphony.

"Nothing."

Morgan tried to stifle a laugh but failed miserably. "Eli, come on. You were so obviously drawing something."

"It doesn't matter."

She stopped and turned him around so that he had to face her, then lifted his chin up to look in his eyes.

"It matters to me."

"It's stupid."

"I've never, for one second, thought your drawings are stupid." Then she added, with her voice lowered because kids were walking around them, "They can open a portal into another world. How could they, like, *ever* be stupid?"

Eli paused, then took the drawing pad from underneath his arm. He started to open it, but was interrupted by a loud voice directed towards the siblings.

"Hey, look! It's the sisters!"

There was a group of three boys and two girls crowding them in a semicircle. They were all laughing. These must have been the kids who had been bullying Eli. The kid Morgan figured to be the leader was as big for his age as Eli was small for his; he had bright red hair and ghostly white skin. Eli shuffled a step towards Morgan, and she was reminded of the day they'd encountered Mahihkan for the first time. It made her feel more protective than she'd felt all day.

"Holy, did you get held back a grade, like, six million times?" she asked the leader.

One of the boys beside the leader laughed. He had messy blond hair, Coke-bottle glasses, a plaid jacket, and ripped black jeans. The leader slapped him on the stomach. The boy made an *oomph* sound.

"Geez, what the heck?" the boy said, holding his stomach.

The leader took a step forward. Morgan and Eli took a step back.

"It's cute that you're trying to protect your sister," he said.

Some kids who were walking by kept walking, some of them a bit faster when they saw what was going on. Some kids who had been walking by stopped and watched, but did nothing.

"Is that seriously your best insult? That he looks like a girl because he has long hair? No wonder you were held back!"

"Shut up or I'll kick your butt too!" the leader warned.

"She's *so* Pocahontas," one of the girls said to the other, who snickered in response.

"I mean, look at her moccasins," the other girl said.

The first girl tapped her hand over her mouth and made a whooping sound, performing a stereotypical war cry. The other girl joined in.

"Wow, *so* original," Morgan said to all of them. "Picking on the Native kid with a braid, making fun of a Native girl by calling her Pocahontas. Find some new material! And by the way, you're wearing Blundstones!" Morgan scoffed at the first girl's footwear. "You're making fun of me? Way to be basic!"

"Stop it," Eli whispered to Morgan.

"You should listen to your sister," the leader said to Morgan. "She's smart for a girl."

"Yeah, listen to your sister," the third boy said, chuckling.

"You making fun of *my brother* for having long hair by calling him a girl is like if I called you Shrek because you're an ugly giant," Morgan said. "But I wouldn't do that because it's super mean."

"You literally just called him that," the boy with messy hair and Coke-bottle glasses said.

"Whoops," Morgan said.

The leader punched a fist into his palm. The group kept moving towards her and Eli. Morgan and Eli kept backing away. Many kids hurried past them, but more kids stopped to watch the show. Morgan noticed some phones up, recording what was happening. Great. This was going to be on social media until the end of time.

The leader gave Morgan a long, angry look, then turned his attention to Eli. He was standing slightly behind her, his drawing pad hugged to his chest.

The leader motioned towards the drawing pad. "What kind of gay stuff are you drawing in that thing?"

"Nothing." Eli's voice was trembling.

"Give it to me." The leader reached for the drawing pad.

"He's not giving it to you, you homophobic jerk!" Morgan said.

"I'll take whatever I want to take," the leader said. "Go ahead and try to stop me."

Morgan felt heat rise in her chest. She wanted to stop him. She wanted to punch him right in his smug, stupid face. She wanted to protect her brother from this, just as she said she would. But she just stood there.

"That's what I thought."

The leader ripped the drawing pad from Eli's arms. The only thing left behind was one lonely sheet of paper, clutched between Eli's thumb and index finger. It was the drawing that he'd been about to show Morgan, torn but mostly intact.

"Give it back!" Eli said, crying.

"*Give it back!*" The second boy imitated Eli.

The third boy fake cried to make fun of Eli's tears.

"You want it?" The leader had the drawing pad gripped in his enormous hands. "Come and get it."

Eli just stood there, like Morgan. Without it, they wouldn't be able to get to Askí tonight. The beings in Misewa would be waiting for them, expecting them, and they wouldn't show up. They wouldn't have any paper big enough to draw an image that could become a portal, and the page he'd torn out already had a drawing on it that Morgan couldn't see. Who knew if it was of the Barren Grounds? Who knew if it was something they could use?

Eli's eyes were pooling with tears. His body was shaking. He wasn't about to try to get the pad again, and she didn't blame him. She wasn't about to either. There were five bullies and only two of them. It was simpler than Misewa Math. She looked at Eli, then at the bullies, then found herself looking at all the spectators. Morgan and Eli were being watched like this was a reality TV show, as though the kids didn't care that she and Eli were getting harassed.

"I didn't think a girl like you would try," the leader said to Eli.

He lunged towards Eli with a fist raised. Eli stumbled backward. Morgan raised her arms in defense, startled by the movement too. The leader laughed, the others laughed along, and then they walked away.

When they were out of sight, Eli, with shaking hands, folded up the piece of paper he'd managed to keep. He put it in his kangaroo pocket, making a square bulge there. A larger version of Morgan's Post-it Note. Morgan took Eli's hands to keep them from shaking. She tried to smile at him, but it came out like a grimace. There was nothing to smile about. All that talk in the bathroom, all those good intentions to protect him, seemed as far away as the North Country.

"Come on," she said. "Let's go home."

He didn't move at first, even when she tugged at his hands. She knew why. They would walk home, but not really. Their home was Misewa, and there would be no Misewa tonight. After what had just happened, that's exactly where they both needed to be. What were they supposed to do now?

NINE

The walk home was quiet, the silence broken only by honking cars, the groan of a city bus, a yapping dog behind a white picket fence, and Morgan and Eli's footsteps. Morgan had her mother's name and phone number folded up and pushed deep into her pocket. Eli had his drawing folded up and pushed into the kangaroo pocket beside his cut hair, severed from his body like a limb.

When they got there, they both went to their rooms.

Dinner was even quieter. Katie and James didn't interrogate them about their gloomy demeanor. They didn't even ask Eli to put his hood down at the dining room table, which normally wouldn't have been acceptable. After giving Morgan her mother's name and phone number that morning, they probably felt it best to give her some space, and Eli by association. That made it easy for her to leave the table early, saying that she didn't feel well. Eli didn't really need an excuse—by now, their foster parents understood that where one went, the other followed.

The night grew dark, but Morgan didn't turn on her bedroom light. She hoped that when Katie or James came up to bed and passed her room, they would see the darkness and keep going, assuming she was asleep. They wouldn't see her sitting on the floor in front of the window, doing nothing but staring out at the streetlight. Finally, she looked away and pulled the Post-it Note from her pocket. She unfolded it, and she saw her mother's name and number again. She wasn't afraid of the dark anymore, but she felt fear when confronted with somebody's contact information.

"Can I come in?"

Morgan whipped around and saw Eli standing at the bedroom door. He'd opened it without her noticing. How long had he been standing there?

She slipped the note into her pocket.

"You kind of already did."

Eli walked all the way inside her room and sat down beside her. They were both leaning against her bed, staring out the window. She didn't know what he'd chosen to focus on, but she looked at the streetlight again until he pulled the drawing out of his kangaroo pocket.

"I've been thinking a lot about what Ochek did for us the first time we went to Misewa," Eli said. "Before he . . ."

"Ochek did a lot for us. You wanna give me a clue?"

"Do you think about him?"

"Of course I do. I think about him all the time. You know I do."

"Do you miss him?"

"Eli, you know I think about Ochek and you know I miss him." She motioned to the sky outside the bedroom window, far past the streetlight. She motioned to the sky as though it were a different sky. Askí's sky. "We go into the Barren Grounds together. We watch for him together. And"—she pushed some loose strands of hair behind her ears—"as much as we miss him, we know that he's still there."

"But he's not." Eli started to unfold the paper, something Morgan had been waiting for since he'd taken the paper out. She'd wondered where Eli was going with all this talk about Ochek. "He's stardust," he said, "and that's all. He's not really there. Not the Ochek we knew anyway."

"We're all stardust, aren't we? You taught me that. You always tell me that Cree people came from the stars, from a hole in the sky or something."

"Those are just stories." The paper was now just folded in half. Eli began to lift the last fold to reveal the drawing he'd saved from the bullies. "They aren't real. I have parents. You have parents. Human parents, not stars."

"Parents," Morgan repeated. Did she have parents? She'd had a mother for two years, that's all she knew. And then she didn't. Did that count as having parents? She fingered the Post-it Note in her pocket.

"Ochek always protected us."

The drawing was in front of them, obstructing their view of the window. It was a pencil illustration of the Barren Grounds—all of Eli's drawings featured the Barren Grounds because the portal opened to it. In the distance, Misewa was visible. That was also typical of his work. If his drawings didn't have either of these things, the portal wouldn't open. They'd tried it one night. They'd stapled an illustration of another world, with different beings, on the wall, and no portal opened to another reality. It was just . . . art on a wall. And, just as he was in the first drawing Eli had made, the one that had opened the portal, Ochek was there front and center, standing in the Barren Grounds, waiting for them.

"I know he did," Morgan said. "I know he protected us, but he can't anymore."

"What if he could?"

Morgan looked more closely at the drawing, and that's when she saw it. The Ochek in the picture wasn't the Ochek they'd known. The courageous, often surly hunter who had taught them so much. Who had, yes, protected them. Who had sacrificed himself to save his village and all of the North Country. The Ochek in this picture was younger. A child. Thinner, shorter, with innocent, almost mischievous eyes. A tiny smirk on his young, furry face. Morgan felt a stab of pain and a sense of deep longing. And oh, how real this Ochek felt. Like she was really there in front of him. Like he was only feet away from her, not in a parallel dimension, in the sky.

"This is amazing," she said.

"What if we could go back in time and actually see him again?" Eli said.

"You want to . . ." Morgan took the drawing from Eli and inspected it thoroughly. "You want to . . . time travel?"

"Yeah," Eli said matter-of-factly.

"Nobody can time travel, on earth or anywhere else." She handed him the picture. "No matter what you draw."

"I thought about going back in time to see Ochek alive, and I saw this. I saw him. I didn't make it up. It came to me like it did when we went to Askí the first time."

"Just because this picture . . . came to you . . . doesn't mean it'll work."

"It has every other time to get to Askí."

"Well, it won't work this time. Come on, Eli. Going back in time? Really? That will *never* work."

"You don't know that."

"Yeah . . . I do."

Morgan saw that she was breaking Eli's heart, but the truth was, even if there was a chance, it felt like the smallest chance, like winning the lottery, or even less than that. That made her feel less guilty about dismissing the idea.

Eli stood and moved to leave, but Morgan got to her feet and grabbed his shoulder.

"Don't you try to leave without me," she warned.

"If it won't work, then what do you care? I won't be going *anywhere*, right?"

"Just drop it, okay? It's false hope! Nothing would happen, and then what? We'd have to say goodbye to him all over again. It's being cruel . . . to *ourselves*."

"I'm sorry, but tell me if I'm wrong. Haven't we been traveling to another reality the last two weeks? Haven't we, somehow, spent, like, two years there? But *this* would never work?"

"We've been going to another reality, Eli. Time travel is another thing entirely."

"It's scientifically possible—I googled it!"

"Google will tell you anything if you want it to! And even if we were somehow able to meet kid Ochek, what's your big plan? Huh? We can't bring him to earth so that he can beat up a bunch of bullies for you. Some evil lab would, like, kidnap him and do experiments on him or something. It happens in movies all the time!"

"Oh, I see. You'll believe movies but not Google?"

"Eli! Stop! Just . . . just . . ." Morgan sat on the bed and lowered her head. She pressed her palms against her forehead and took some deep breaths. Each time she'd said the word "just," she'd grown quieter. Now she whispered, "Just let it go."

Eli sat, more like collapsed, beside her. "I just want to feel protected. That's all. I thought maybe—"

"He could protect you, like he protected us before."

"Yeah."

Morgan put her arm around Eli.

"I can . . . I *will* . . . do a better job of protecting you. But we can't . . ." Morgan trailed off as an image of her mother popped into her head, and the man and woman who had torn her from her mother's arms. She often imagined how different things would have been if she hadn't been abducted. How she would have been rocked in her mother's arms. How she would have played with her mother's hair. How she would never have had to hear that word, *Kiskisitotaso*, as a warning to never forget herself. But all of that was just a fantasy, and she knew it. "We can't change the past. We can't go back in time."

"No." Eli stood again, and this time he left. Morgan didn't try to stop him. When he was gone, walking across the hallway towards his bedroom, Morgan heard him say under his breath, "I guess we can't."

Even with Eli gone, Morgan kept thinking about the stupid drawing. She was staring out the window, thinking about time travel. About Ochek. Then, about her mother.

That's when, without realizing it, Morgan found herself typing in Jenny Trout's phone number. Her thumb hesitated over the call button for a second, then she pressed the green circle with the white phone icon. One ring. Two rings. Three. Four. Five. Too many. *Thump, thump, thump, thump, thump, thump, thump.* Morgan's heart pounded a million beats for every ring. Then came a voice.

"*Tansi.*"

A woman's voice. By the sound of it, an older woman. Was it her mother? It had to be. Morgan paused, not knowing how to begin. What was there to say? Only everything, about all the tiny moments that her mother had missed. What was there to ask? Everything too, but mostly: Why had she missed all those moments? What could have happened to make her decide to give up her daughter?

"*Tansi,*" the woman said again. "Hello?"

Morgan's heart skipped when she almost, *almost*, said hello back. But she didn't. Instead of saying one word, she ended the call. The phone dropped to the ground and settled. She was transfixed by the cold, black device. It was a blackness that Morgan felt she could get sucked into. In the silence, her mother's voice replayed to the sound of her beating heart. *Thump, thump, thump, thump, thump, thump, thump.* Not the same word she'd heard before, imagined before, so many times. *Kiskisitotaso.* It was simpler now but felt just as important. *Tansi.*

Knock. Knock.

"Hello," Morgan said.

"Morgan?" Katie took a step into the bedroom. "Everything okay?"

Morgan quickly wiped a tear from her cheek. She'd only just felt the cool trail of it on her skin.

"Yeah, fine."

She did another wipe with both hands to ensure there were no more stray tears, then forced a smile. It must have been as unconvincing as it felt. Katie came all the way in and sat on the foot of the bed.

"I heard you and Eli arguing."

"Oh, that?" Morgan found the streetlight and fixed her eyes on it. "That was just brother and sister stuff. Not a big deal. We worked it out."

"Good. 'Brother and sister stuff.' That's *really* good. I mean, not that you're arguing, but, you know."

"Yeah, I know."

Morgan wanted her foster mother to leave. If she didn't look at her, maybe Katie would get the message. But Katie stubbornly stayed where she was. When she eventually moved, it wasn't to leave, just to lean forward. Morgan took this as a signal that Katie wasn't going anywhere until she told her what was really wrong. Morgan couldn't decide whether to be annoyed or comforted by that.

"Did you actually ask her if I could call? Did she say yes?" Morgan looked at the orange streetlight and only the orange streetlight. What she saw in her mind, however, was Jenny Trout and only Jenny Trout. Her face, her hair, her voice. *Tansi.*

"Not exactly, but—"

"*Not exactly*? Who's the one in grade eight here?" Morgan swiveled her entire body towards Katie. "She either did or she didn't, and if she didn't, then why'd you even give me her number in the first place?"

Katie looked startled by Morgan's aggressiveness and almost fell off the bed. She put her hand on her chest. "I asked for the number when you first came here, just in case—"

"Just in case you wanted to get rid of me, and thought that you'd pawn me off on my mother, who didn't want me in the first place, so why would she want me now?"

"No. No, Morgan." Katie was on the verge of tears. She may have been crying already, it was hard to tell. It was dark in the room, and Morgan's own tears blurred her vision. "That's not it at all. We'd *never* pawn you off, or try to get rid of you. We just thought one day it would be best, if it worked out, that you talk to your mother."

"What did you want me to do? Call Jenny Trout out of the blue, like, more than a decade after I got taken away and just be, like, 'Hey, Mom, what's up?' I mean, *really*?" Morgan slid off the bed to the floor in a heap and covered her face with her hands. She wanted to scream but instead kept completely silent.

Katie, too, was silent. It was so quiet that Morgan was certain she could hear Eli breathing. He'd probably heard the whole exchange between her and Katie, just as Katie had heard her and Eli arguing. They were a bunch of eavesdroppers.

"I'm sorry," Katie said. "It seemed like the right thing to do, but you're right, I shouldn't have just . . . I can't stop screwing things up, can I?"

Had Katie screwed up? Morgan wasn't sure. Yes, she probably should have given Jenny Trout a heads-up that her daughter might call after over a decade. But was that what Morgan was really mad about? Was she mad at all? Or was she scared that a real-life conversation with her mother could never live up to the imaginary ones she'd had the last two weeks. Scared that the memories she'd had recently about the day she was taken were somehow wrong. That she'd always wanted it to be true that her mother wanted her all along. And what if her mother hung up on her the minute she said, *Hey, Mom, it's me, Morgan.* Maybe it was all of those things. Her palms were wet from tears.

"It would be worse if you were screwing up for different reasons." Morgan took her hands away from her face. "If that makes sense."

"It does." Katie managed a faint smile.

"I just want to be alone for a bit, if that's okay."

"Of course it's okay." Katie got up and paused at the doorway. "I don't want you to stay up late tonight, okay? You need your rest. So no attic, got it? I don't want you guys up there all the time."

"Good night," Morgan said after Katie was already gone. She could have a conversation with Katie, but couldn't say even one word to Jenny Trout. Still on the floor, she shook her head. "You're such a loser. No wonder she got rid of you."

From where she was now, she couldn't see the streetlight. She could see the tree in front of the house on the boulevard, and past it, the night sky. It was a clear night. Unusually clear for the city. She could see the stars like she was out in the country. The North Country. Where the stars were bright like flashlights. Like torches burning to welcome her home. She could see the Big Dipper constellation, the earth counterpart of Ochekatchakosuk. Its bowl, its crooked handle. Its tail. Ochek's tail. Broken by Mason's arrow. Ochek, placed in the sky to honor his sacrifice.

Morgan got up from the floor, crossed the hallway, and found Eli sitting on his bed with the drawing of young Ochek resting on his lap.

"Alright," she said. "Let's try it."

TEN

Morgan and Eli stayed in their own bedrooms and listened for their foster parents until there was not a sound to be heard. Morgan kind of liked that Katie and James behaved like a cute old couple. It was cuter still because they weren't really old—maybe mid-thirties, tops, Morgan guessed. They bickered like grandparents but never really fought. Their fights were more like good-natured teasing. When they were annoyed at each other, it felt like good-natured annoyance. They were just good-natured, Morgan supposed, which made her feel lucky to have them as foster parents, because even when they screwed up, they meant well.

And just like that old couple, at some point early in the evening, Katie and James walked up the stairs together, their footsteps almost synchronized. The door to the stairwell closed, and immediately afterward, their bedroom door was shut too. At that point, Morgan knew it wouldn't be long before James was snoring, which meant it would be safe for her and Eli to make their way to the attic.

Morgan waited, and listened, but for an agonizingly long time there was no snoring. Were Katie and James staying up . . . talking? This wasn't typical. If they didn't fall asleep straightaway, Katie would be reading, James watching an action movie. *They're probably talking about me and Eli*, Morgan thought. *They're probably trying to figure out what to do with us because we've been so weird today.*

Curiosity got Morgan off the floor before it was time to leave for Misewa. She leaned into the hallway to hear better. It didn't help. Katie and James's conversation sounded like mumbling. She didn't dare go any closer. If they heard her up, if they heard just one creak from the floorboards, they might want to talk to her, or stay up later listening for her, and then she and Eli would have to wait even longer to go to Misewa.

Luckily for her, Katie and James's conversation ended unexpectedly and abruptly. Morgan remained still for several minutes, until she was absolutely certain that Katie and James were fast asleep. Then she walked across the hallway and into Eli's bedroom. She found her brother lying in bed with his arms crossed behind his head and the drawing on his lap.

"Ready?" she whispered.

"Yeah," he whispered back.

He got off the bed and followed her out of his bedroom to the door that led to the attic. She gripped the doorknob, turned it slowly, and pulled the door open without a creak. They climbed to the attic using the sides of the treads, because the middle areas groaned under any weight and they couldn't afford to make a sound. Katie had explicitly told Morgan that they weren't to go up to the attic tonight.

If they got busted, there would be no Misewa, no Ochek, and nothing good after such a rotten day. They got to the top of the stairs without a hitch, and with the extra space now separating them from their foster parents' bedroom, they could make a bit of noise.

"Almost there," Morgan whispered.

"This is going to work, you know," Eli whispered.

"I know it is."

"How? I was just thinking positively."

"I see." Morgan lightly punched Eli on the arm so she didn't actually hurt him, because he might yelp, and a yelp would be too loud. "Jerk."

Eli rubbed his arm dramatically. "You didn't answer my question, *jerk*."

"I know it's going to work because it has to after the day we've had. It's karma."

They went to the door of their secret room, and Morgan reached for the knob.

"What did we do for good karma?"

"Well, *I* did something for good karma, and I'm sure it'll rub off on you."

Morgan had kept her hand on the knob and now pulled the door open. Standing in the middle of their secret room was James, his cellphone flashlight on to illuminate the small space. He shook his head with a tight-lipped smile.

"I'm not really happy catching you two up here," James said.

"You were just waiting in the attic?" Morgan asked. "That's kind of weird."

"We know you hang out in this room, and we've been letting it go," James said. "But judging by how you both looked this morning, you've been hanging out here too often, and too late. We didn't give you unlimited access. You were upset one day and—"

"Okay, I got it," Morgan said. "We don't need to rehash my meltdown, thanks."

"How long were you just going to stand here?" Eli asked.

"I was listening," James explained. "Katie and I agreed that we weren't going to allow you to come up here tonight. We know you were up here last night, despite what you told us. When I heard Morgan go into your room, I thought I'd head you guys off."

"Well played," Morgan said.

James walked out of the secret room and shut the door behind him. All three of them were standing at the top of the stairs in the attic. It was a scenario Morgan had dreaded since discovering the portal. What now? Would he close off the door forever? Nail boards across it? Have the construction guys, the next time they decided to show up, get rid of the door entirely? Would he have them put up a wall and close them off from Misewa forever? She felt ready to cry, and in the light coming from the window, she could see tears in Eli's eyes as well.

"What now?" Eli asked.

"Yeah," Morgan said. "You're not going to, like, lock us out of our room, are you?"

James looked at Morgan, then Eli, then Morgan, then Eli. He looked the most serious Morgan had ever seen him. But then, as deadly serious as James had been, he put one hand on Morgan's shoulder, one hand on Eli's shoulder, and smiled.

"I got you, though, didn't I?"

"Yeah." Morgan was too relieved to be mad at his fake angry face. In any other moment, his fake angry face would've made her furious. More furious than the happy breakfast face he'd made her once with eggs, two strips of bacon, hash browns, and a perfectly quartered orange. "You got us."

"You probably thought, because you're a rebellious teenager, that you'd be the one who's great at sneaking around, then *poof*, James pulls *that* off."

"Please don't talk about yourself in the third person. You're not Elmo, you're a real person."

"*That's* weird," Eli agreed.

"Anyway." With his hands still on their shoulders, James guided them towards the stairs and downstairs.

The three of them stood in the second-floor hallway. Morgan and Eli had been caught, fair and square. The real consequence of getting caught, however, was just starting to dawn on Morgan. No Misewa. What were they to do? Wait until James was actually sleeping, then try to sneak up again?

"Now," James said, "I don't want to stay up all night watching the stairs to make sure you two don't try to go off to that room again, okay? I've got surgery tomorrow and I don't want to mess up because I'm too tired."

"You mean, like, leave a scalpel in somebody's body or something?" Morgan asked.

"Something like that."

"Well, I wouldn't want to be responsible for a grave medical error and a possible malpractice lawsuit," she muttered.

"Listen," James said. "In all seriousness. Can I count on you two? Please?"

Eli nodded, but his shoulders dropped. He was devastated.

Morgan didn't say anything. She didn't nod her head. She was weighing options while James and Eli watched her. *Could* he count on her? She could say that he could, but cross her fingers behind her back. She could say that he could, then, when he was sleeping, sneak up with Eli and enter the portal to Misewa and see if Eli's plan to time travel would really work. And if they stayed, like, a week, they'd be back in one hour and never get caught.

But then Katie's face popped into Morgan's mind, with that sad look she'd had earlier, saying that she screwed up all the time. What if they lied, snuck up to the attic, and went through the portal? What if Katie and James woke up and found them out of their beds? What if they went to the attic and discovered the portal? What would happen? *Well,* she thought, *they could have heart attacks. It's not every day you find a portal to another reality.* But James was a cardiologist, so maybe they'd survive? Morgan shook her head at the thought. *Don't be stupid.* The worst part was this: if Katie and James discovered that she and Eli had gone to the attic after promising not to—whether they found the portal or not—Katie would feel even more like a screwup. And Morgan would feel even more like a jerk.

"Morgan?" James prompted. "Can I count on you?"

"Yeah. You can count on me."

"Alright." James yawned. "I trust you, or I'm too tired to *not* trust you. Good night, kids."

James disappeared into his bedroom and shut the door. Eli and Morgan looked at each other.

"We're still going to go, right?" he whispered.

She shook her head. "No, we're not going."

"What? Why not?"

"It's too risky. What if we get caught again? Thank goodness he didn't catch us while we had the portal open."

Eli looked back and forth like he didn't know where to go or what to do. "So what's your plan, then? Wait until tomorrow night? Are we even going to try to time travel? We can just get more paper at school."

"Yes, we're going to try to time travel," Morgan said. "We both want to see Ochek, don't we?"

"We do, but if this works"—Eli held up the drawing—"Arik and everybody else in present day are going to wait even longer to see us again."

"I'm getting mixed messages here, brother. Fine. We can totally scrap the whole time travel thing. I'm kind of invested now, but hey, at least, you know, we have Ochek with us in the sky at night."

"I want to try, it's just . . ."

Morgan gave him a hug, even kissed him on top of his head. "Look. It's not a big deal if they have to wait for us a bit longer than usual."

"*Way* longer than usual."

"Well, they went their whole lives without us before we got there, didn't they?"

"I guess so."

"They'll be okay. Arik, Muskwa, all of them."

"*I* won't be, though," Eli said.

"Yes, you will be," Morgan said.

Eli pushed away from her. His eyes had never looked bigger or sadder. "Past or present, tomorrow night is such a long time from now."

Morgan made a *pfft* sound, as though the idea of waiting until tomorrow night was silly. As though the idea of waiting until tomorrow night was completely out of the question. The fact was, she'd come up with a foolproof plan in the last couple of minutes.

"Who said anything about going tomorrow *night*?" she asked. "I'm not waiting that long . . . I don't know about you."

"I don't get it," Eli said. "We can't go tonight and there's school tomorrow."

Morgan faked a cough. "I think I'm coming down with something."

Eli's face smoothed out as he realized what she meant, and then he smiled broadly.

"We're for real going to play hooky?" he whispered excitedly.

"Yeah, we are," she said. "Both of us."

ELEVEN

In the morning, it didn't take much to convince Katie that both Morgan and Eli were sick. Morgan sensed that Katie was still being a bit wary with her, maybe because of the business with the Post-it Note, so even if she'd had her doubts, she likely wouldn't have challenged Morgan. And they hadn't seemed right at dinner the night before. Morgan had even said she felt sick as an excuse to leave supper early, inadvertently making her illness look less sudden and supporting the plan to stay home from school today. And if Morgan was sick, Katie mused aloud before leaving for work, it wasn't out of the realm of possibility that Eli would be sick too. They spent most of their time together, and some of that time was in a small, musty, cold attic room. Plus, Eli had slept in his hoodie, had diligently kept his hood up, and to Katie and James it probably looked as though he had the chills, not that he was hiding shortened hair.

"Text me right away if you feel worse," she said in the hallway, between their bedroom doors. "I'll come right home."

"We will," Morgan promised.

And then, just moments later, Katie was gone.

Morgan jumped out of bed, ran into Eli's room, and, with new hope, picked up the drawing. There was the Barren Grounds and its desolate landscape stretched out before them. There was the forest lining the horizon with its diverse population of trees—jack pine, tamarack, balsam fir, white spruce, paper birch. Even from a great distance, it called to her and was beautiful. There was Misewa at the edge of the trees, its seven longhouses encircling the Council Hut, the lights from inside the dwellings a beacon for them—but Morgan now could find her way there blindfolded, just by memory and feel. And there was young Ochek, sitting on the ground facing her, paws at his sides flat against the earth, legs stretched out. What was he doing? Morgan decided that he was waiting for them.

They climbed the stairs to the attic and went inside their secret room, closing the door behind them. It was usually dark when they went there at night, and even now, in the morning, it wasn't much brighter.

Morgan was nervous—what if the picture didn't work? They would have to lie around all day, disappointed and bored. And worse, there would be no Misewa that night either, because they wouldn't be at school to get another drawing pad! Or what if it did work, but not in the way they hoped, and instead they entered Askí in the present? Ochek would be in the sky at night, and that would be the only way they would ever see him again. At least that would be better than not seeing him at all. Or maybe the picture would work as planned, and Morgan and Eli would see

Ochek again, young and alive. He wouldn't have met the siblings yet, but no matter. They could get to know him all over again.

Morgan passed Eli her phone. He turned on the flashlight and pointed it at the slanting wall. She pressed the drawing against the wood with one hand, and with the other she positioned the staple gun over the first corner of Eli's creation.

"This will work," she said.

"I think so," he said.

"You're supposed to say that it'll work!"

"It'll work."

"Too late. I've contributed all the karma and the positive thoughts."

"Let's hope that's enough, then."

Thwack.

A staple shot into the wood and fastened the top right corner of the drawing to the slanting wall. A cool breeze pushed through the thin white paper, as soft as a child blowing out a candle. Loose strands of Morgan's hair swayed in front of her eyes.

Thwack.

A staple embedded into the wood through the top left corner of the paper. The bottom of the paper kicked out towards Morgan, and she flattened it. She pushed hair away from her eyes with her forearm. Ochek still hadn't come to life. He remained a figure in pencil.

"It's working," Eli said.

"Duh," Morgan said. "The air feels like autumn over there."

"As long as it isn't winter."

"You'd go to Askí no matter how cold it was."

"Yeah, but I'd rather stay there when it isn't cold, if I have a choice."

"Me too," she admitted.

Thwack.

There was only one more staple to go. The air was refreshing, and it filled the room. Morgan welcomed the goose pimples popping up all over her body. She couldn't help but smile, even as she worried that Ochek would disappear when the final staple was in.

"Here we go," she said.

Morgan pressed the staple gun against the bottom left corner of the drawing. She let go of the paper with her other hand, and as it hung at her side, Eli took it and squeezed. The moment of truth.

Thwack.

The portal opened. Morgan peered over the edge, and there was the North Country in all of its beauty in front of them. The southern woods against the horizon. Misewa. The Barren Grounds. And several feet from the Great Tree, standing up now, was a smaller, younger Ochek. Morgan started crying from happiness. There were so many tears that she couldn't wipe them away fast enough. Her cheeks were soaked. Her hands were soaked. Eli was crying too. He was wiping his face against her shoulder. Ochek was alive. It was a miracle. It had worked. They'd gone back in time.

"That has to be him. He's exactly like you saw him." Morgan barely managed to catch enough breath to get the words out. "You brought him back, Eli."

"No, I didn't," Eli whispered. "He just hasn't gone anywhere yet."

Morgan took a deep, calming breath. Ochek was walking towards them. He had tan-colored pants, a dark green hooded top with short sleeves, and a satchel strapped over his shoulder.

"Tansi," he said.

Ochek sounded nothing like the Ochek they knew. He sounded young—young enough, if he were a human, to be a kid in Morgan's class. Whenever this was, the long White Time hadn't come yet. The man, Mason, hadn't entered Askí to join the community and then almost destroy it with his greed.

"Tansi?" he said again.

He was annoyed and impatient but, interestingly, not shocked to see two human beings sticking their heads into Askí from another world. Surprised maybe, but not shocked. *Tansi.* Morgan hadn't known what to say to her mother earlier. She didn't know what to say to Ochek now. And how they must have looked to him. Two human kids crying their eyes out while peeking out from inside the Great Tree.

"Hey," she said, and she wiped her eyes again.

He was standing right in front of the tree, and he leaned forward, close to them. Morgan looked into his endless black eyes. He looked kind of like Rocket Raccoon from *Guardians of the Galaxy*, only bigger, and a fisher. She looked at him very carefully, as carefully as he was looking at them. *Fishers and raccoons weren't all that different*, she thought.

"Oh, you speak *those* words." Ochek sighed and extended a

paw. "Well, are you coming or what, humans? Astum. I can't be in this space much longer."

Morgan and Eli traded a look as though they needed to decide if they were going to go, but there was no hesitation. They'd been longing to see Ochek ever since he'd sacrificed himself. Now he was there, just feet away, his paw extended to help them through the portal like it was a normal everyday occurrence.

"We're coming."

Morgan reached through the portal and clasped Ochek's forearm. She couldn't help but smile when she felt his fingers press against her skin. He was real. He was really real. She didn't want him to ever let go.

TWELVE

As soon as the children were through the portal, and they'd moved away from the area where earth's time spilled into Askí, Morgan lunged forward with the sort of quickness she'd seen from Arik and wrapped her arms around Ochek. She pressed her cheek against his shoulder. Eli soon had one arm around Ochek and another around Morgan. His face was against the animal being's chest. Ochek let out an *oof* after the hug attack, and decided, Morgan figured, to allow the children to hug him for as long as they wanted to. He would tell them later that he let them because something was familiar about the children, and besides, their joy was catching.

When the embrace finally ended, a silence stretched on long enough to be awkward, but Morgan would gladly take an awkward moment with Ochek over any moment without him.

"Is that how you greet one another where you come from?" Ochek asked.

"Depends on who you're greeting, I guess," she said. "In some places they kiss on the cheek."

"Gross," Ochek said. "Hugging was fine." He surveyed the sky. It was getting darker with each passing moment. "I should get back. My father won't be happy if I'm not home soon and I've already been around the Great Tree too long. Time is weird around it."

"How's that?" Morgan asked, feeling as though she ought to play dumb.

"It's like when you're around it, everywhere else in the North Country speeds up," Ochek explained. "It's odd, but then again, everything about the tree's odd. I mean, you both just came out of it."

"Good point," Eli said.

Ochek started to walk into the Barren Grounds. "Do you want to come see my village?"

"That'd be awesome, if we're allowed," Morgan said.

"I don't think anybody would mind."

What a change, Morgan thought, from how they'd been greeted on their first visit, when animals had thrown snowballs at them and shouted at them to leave. She knew they'd been angry because of Mason's betrayal, and because they didn't trust any humans. But it was still odd to arrive as strangers and be welcomed so readily. It made her realize how much damage had been done by one selfish man.

Before leaving for Misewa, the siblings remembered that they had to close the portal, as they always did. This meant, to Ochek's chagrin, going near the Great Tree again. Of course, there were no clothes for Morgan and Eli to change into, and more importantly, no pieces of plywood leaned up against the tree, ready to cover the hole. There was no hammer, either. Morgan promised it would take just a minute, which still meant around an hour on Askí, but the animal being decided to wait for them. Eli hurriedly climbed back through the hole and came out again with pieces of plywood, nails, and another hammer.

"Thank god nobody comes to work on the attic," Morgan said while they worked to close the hole. "What would happen if they showed up and discovered all their hammers were gone? They might go looking for one."

"And find the portal," Eli said. "We have to remember to bring it back when we leave."

"Totally." For some reason, a construction guy finding Askí seemed much worse to Morgan than Katie or James finding it.

As promised, in no more than a minute, the portal had been covered and the three of them entered the Barren Grounds. Still, despite Morgan and Eli's efficiency, the sky had sprinted into darkness.

"Look at how late it is!" Ochek lamented. "I'm going to be in *so* much trouble with my father!"

He kicked at the ground and dirt flew into the air only to be blown back into his face by the wind, which was always stronger across the desolate land between the northern and southern woods. The children laughed. Ochek wiped the dirt off his fur, looking embarrassed.

It wasn't long into the journey when a question struck Morgan. Ochek had been looking at them curiously since they'd arrived in this younger version of Askí. He felt a connection to them; it was in his eyes. But how? And why hadn't he freaked out when she and Eli appeared from within the Great Tree? He'd calmly said "Tansi" to them, as though humans climbing out of the portal in the Great Tree was an everyday occurrence. So, was it? Had she and Eli been here before, even further in the past, to see an even younger Ochek? So young that he wouldn't remember them, but he'd feel that unspoken, indescribable familiarity? The same one she'd felt standing before the northern woods on her first visit?

"Is the Great Tree, like, a portal that opens all the time?" Morgan asked loudly because Ochek was walking fast.

Ochek shrugged. "I don't know. Maybe."

"Do you know any, I guess, Great Tree stories?"

"Everybody does," Ochek said.

"Can you tell us one?"

"Yeah, sure," Ochek answered without breaking stride.

Morgan was used to hearing stories sitting at the fireside, not from a storyteller who was speed-walking. It was hard to hear him. She and Eli quickened their pace to remain within earshot.

"The story goes that a bunch of villagers went to the northern woods to hunt, right? They decided to camp at the Great Tree because, I guess, they were tired. So, they went to sleep. Because, like I said, they were tired. Well, in the night, Mistapew came—he's a giant who's super quiet, like *deadly* quiet—and he took the soul of Kihiw, the eagle. Mistapew takes souls like a bear takes berries. Anyway, Kihiw was an Elder in Misewa. Then, the story goes, the big giant warned all the others never to come back."

Morgan and Eli looked at each other. It was so weird to hear teenage Ochek tell the same story that older Ochek had told them. He'd become a more poetic storyteller over the years, but Morgan, at least, preferred this version. And it wasn't over yet.

"Since that time, over the past hundreds of years, long after Kihiw's body had wasted away, the Great Tree has been magical or something. I mean, we in Misewa have always considered it to be sacred, but, you know, that doesn't mean *magic.* From time to time, to answer your question, humans have come through portals in the North Country. I don't know about that one specifically, but you two aren't the first to come here through one, let's put it that way."

"Have *you* seen humans come through one before?" It was the question Morgan really wanted answered.

"Nah," Ochek said. "But I've heard stories about that too, and . . ." Ochek stopped, then turned to the humans, and for one second, only one, his eyes hinted at the old, wise hunter he would one day become. "The stories we tell here aren't fantasies. They're real, all of them."

Then the old, wise hunter was gone in a blink. Ochek shrugged, spun around to face the direction Misewa was in, and kept walking. He even began to whistle a song that Morgan had never heard before, that she did not feel a connection to.

She thought back to what Ochek had said: the stories they told here were real, all of them. If she and Eli had been here before, there would have been stories about them too. In their present, Morgan and Eli's, there most certainly were stories about them. Their journey with Arik and Ochek had made it onto the walls of the Council Hut. It felt like having a championship trophy in a glass display case.

"We need to talk about the whole time travel thing," Morgan said quietly, once Ochek was well ahead of them and out of earshot.

"What *about* the whole time travel thing? We're here," Eli said. "It worked."

"Yeah, it worked, obviously, but . . ." The whole idea of time travel was dizzying, even more now that they'd actually done it. Morgan worked hard to make sense of all her thoughts on the subject as they swirled around in her brain like snowflakes in a blizzard. But it was an impossible task. She was sure of only one thing, because in every book and movie the same conversation took place whenever time travel was involved. "We have to figure out what the actual rules of time travel are, don't you think?"

"I guess?"

"Okay, so, here's how I see it," Morgan said. "There are two types of time travel scenarios. There's *Back to the Future,* of course, and all the other movies like that one. Like—"

"You know, I watch movies too," Eli said, "and by now it's kind of boring when they start discussing time travel."

"Yeah, but isn't that important? What if we could really change things by accident?"

"Well, we're not going to come across our past or future selves, and that's the main time travel thing, so why don't we just not tell them what's going to happen, because whatever happened has to happen?"

"Yeah," Morgan grumbled, "Muskwa told me that. All those struggles made them stronger, and it made *us* stronger, and all that crap."

"It made us stronger?" Eli said. To demonstrate otherwise, he flipped his hood off to reveal his shortened hair, as if she might have forgotten. "I'm not strong."

"Yes, you are. You can't control bullies." Morgan thought about how she'd hung up on her mother. "And we've all done things that make us feel weak."

Eli pulled the hood back over his hair. "Right."

"I *am* right, and also"—she took his hand and started swinging it, trying to kick-start some positivity—"we just kind of but not really solved time travel!"

"By saying that whatever happened has to happen?"

"Exactly. Don't spoil it; we're clearly geniuses."

Eli tried to hide his grin, but he smiled, so they walked on through the Barren Grounds in good spirits. The usually difficult trip across the desolate plains seemed to pass quickly as a result. With each step, they felt more excitement, and thought less and less about bullies and phone calls cut short.

Soon they were entering Misewa, but not the Misewa they'd come to know.

There were still only seven longhouses that encircled the Council Hut. There were still wooden racks outside of the longhouses. But the seven longhouses weren't the only dwellings. Scattered about the village, although never encroaching into the circle around the Council Hut, were teepees. Warm, flickering orange light came from the flapped entrances to these structures, and smoke rose from the openings at the top where the poles met and extended towards the sky like fingers. In the trees, there were nest-like treehouses. Small, but not as small as birdhouses. They were more like something built for a toddler, if a parent were ever crazy enough to let their toddler up into a tree so high. Wigwams, Morgan decided, were what they resembled, dwellings that she had seen in textbooks. They were made out of sticks and what looked like bark, and Morgan quickly counted seven of them.

The wooden racks were covered with meat drying out to be eaten now or preserved and consumed by the villagers over the winter months. They wanted for nothing, and there was a hum to the village that was bursting with life, a joyous feeling that bubbled in Morgan's chest. Something that could be felt but not seen. A feeling that she had never felt in Misewa, even many months after the Green Time had returned at last. A warmth that no fire could provide. It was in the muffled voices rising from the dwellings like smoke. The songs from some of them. The beat of the drum that flowed through the air, a sound that you could breathe in. Morgan's heart matched the rhythm. She felt it in her chest. She felt it in her lungs.

Still, it was bittersweet to be there, because, despite the longhouses, the teepees, the houses high up in the trees, despite the meat racks, the rising smoke, the cracks of orange light, despite the hum and the beat of the drum, she knew that one day, sooner or later, it would all end. It would end, and many of the villagers here, villagers she had yet to meet, would end too. They would die. Their teepees would be taken down. The wigwams would fall from the security of their branches. The meat racks would empty as stores of food dwindled. The lights would stay, the smoke would continue to rise, but the hum she felt now would leave, along with the green grass and swift waters and four-legged creatures.

She felt that in her chest too.

Morgan found herself holding Eli's hand tighter than ever as they followed Ochek all the way to the door of his long-house. He put his paw on the wood and began to push the door open, but before entering he turned around. He bared his teeth in a grimace, and Morgan realized how worried he was about coming home late.

"So, here we are." Ochek's voice was shaky and cracking. "Welcome to Misewa."

THIRTEEN

Ochek pushed the door and it creaked open, which was not helpful if he was hoping to sneak into the longhouse. In the end, it didn't matter. His parents were sitting on either side of the fire waiting for him. They didn't even notice Morgan and Eli at first, with their eyes trained on their son. His father was the spitting image of him; if Morgan had seen his father first, if he'd been the one by the Great Tree, she would have mistaken him for Ochek. Ochek's father looked to be about Ochek's age when the great hunter passed away, maybe a bit older. Gray freckled his otherwise dark brown fur. He wore light brown pants that were held up by rope or sinew and a black top with long sleeves. Ochek mother's wore dark green capri pants and a short-sleeved beige top.

"Tansi, Nipapa, Nimama," Ochek said hesitantly, and he ventured farther into the living room, towards the fire.

His parents rose to their feet. They were all of similar height, his father slightly taller. Morgan and Eli stood at the open door and watched Ochek begin to explain where he'd been.

Morgan turned to Eli and said quietly, "So, unless 'Nipapa' means 'older fisher,' I guess not all animals are named the Cree word for whatever animal they are."

"No." Eli shook his head and chuckled lightly. "That's not his name. 'Nipapa' means 'my father' in Cree. And 'Nimama' means—"

"My mother."

"Ehe. Good job."

"Yeah," Morgan said exaggeratedly, and she patted Eli on the back. "Just call me Captain Obvious."

"Well, now you know the words anyway."

"They wouldn't all be called Ochek, though, right?" Morgan looked over Ochek's parents carefully, imagining a typical day with the family of fishers where a villager called out, "Ochek!" and all three of them turned around. How annoying would that be? "Maybe it's something like Thing One and Thing Two. I mean, not many of the villagers are called anything other than what they are in Cree." Morgan racked her brain. "Yapéw?"

"No, because remember he's still named after a moose, just a bull moose," Eli pointed out.

"Yeah, you're right," Morgan said. "Oh!" She snapped her fingers. "Casey." She fist-pumped. "Boom."

"We just started calling her that, and then everybody else did," Eli said. "Fox is makésiw. Casey."

"Okay, okay, okay." Morgan crossed her arms. "*Fine.* It's just *you* that's called something other than what animal, or living being, they are."

"And you."

Morgan could still hear Ochek saying her name, for the first time, just before he died. It meant that, after all they'd been through together, he trusted her. Sadness filled her, but only for a moment, because there he was in front of her, no matter the age, and she planned to enjoy their time with him to the fullest. There'd be time for sadness after they left.

"Maybe they're Ochek Junior and Ochek Senior?" But there was his mother as well. "And Mama Ochek?"

Eli didn't offer a response. He was looking blankly at Morgan, who was curious about her brother's facial expression for only a moment before realizing why he'd clammed up.

"They're not talking anymore, are they?" Morgan whispered.

Eli shook his head. His eyes darted towards the figures by the fire, then back to Morgan. He was wide-eyed with anxiety.

"They're looking at us, aren't they?"

Eli nodded.

Morgan swallowed, and in the silence, it was the loudest swallow in the history of the world. She'd hoped to make a good impression on them so that they'd want her and Eli to stay, and how long had they been listening to her and Eli guess what their names might be? How ridiculous did they think the siblings were? Had it ruined their chances?

"What do we do?" she asked through her teeth, as if she were practicing ventriloquism.

"I don't know." Eli spoke the same way.

"Come in here, young ones," said Ochek's father.

"Oh god," Morgan said.

"I guess we go there," Eli said.

Ochek's father's tone commanded respect, but at the same time wasn't demanding. You wanted to listen to him, and the children did. They entered the dwelling, walked across the room, and stopped. There they were, standing before the family of fishers, who were on the other side of the fire. Morgan and Eli stood silently; Morgan didn't think they should be the first ones to speak, especially since they'd just made fools of themselves. Or, more accurately, Morgan had made a fool of herself.

Ochek's father was sizing them up, she could tell. Had he met humans before? If so, were they the Mason kind or the Morgan and Eli kind? That mattered. That could mean whether they stayed or not. Morgan tried to stand straight and look strong but humble. Respectful. Out of the corner of her eye, she saw Eli trying to throw out the same vibe.

"Tansi, children," Ochek's father said.

"Tansi," Eli said.

"Hello," Morgan said, but then corrected herself, because this was a word she knew and felt she should use. "Tansi."

"You speak in the good words," Ochek's father said to Eli. "And I take it that you do not," he said to Morgan.

"She's learning," Eli explained.

"Ehe," Morgan said. "I am."

Morgan looked around the living area to see how different it was from the one she had come to know so well. It was still a modest room, with its firepit and a bench on either side of it, a shuttered window that looked out over the Barren Grounds, and preserved foods, medicines, cutlery, plates, and cups on shelves. There were two dirty plates on the ground by the fire; Ochek's parents hadn't been so worried that they'd skipped dinner, so Ochek couldn't have been in that much trouble. One difference was glaring: the unblemished wooden walls. Not one notch in them to indicate a day spent in the White Time. There had been no suffering through an unending White Time. Not yet.

"How did you come to be here, Iskwésis?" Ochek's father asked.

"Wait a minute." Morgan was unwilling to be called just "Girl" again for however long until they trusted her. She'd worked too hard to be called Morgan in the future. Or present. Whatever it was from when she was.

"What is it, young one?" asked Ochek's mother, who had a strong and fluid voice, like the swift water that ran through the southern woods.

"It's just that, I thought we'd greet each other properly first. I mean, I'm not just 'Girl' in the good words, just like I doubt everybody here calls you Nipapa, because you're not everybody's father, right? I have a name."

Eli cleared his throat. "I'm Eli."

Ochek's father chuckled, not at all annoyed by Morgan. This relieved her. "What do they call you, Iskwésis? I'd be happy to call you by your name."

"Morgan," she said proudly. "Thank you. Ekosani."

Ochek's father, in turn, looked proud to hear the good words come from her mouth, though he'd only just met her. "They call me Mihko."

"And I'm Nikamon," Ochek's mother said. "You can call me Nicky."

Morgan felt warm in her chest, in a positive way. To call Ochek's mother by a nickname felt like an honor. And that reminded her of Arik, short for Arikwachas. For a moment, she thought of their old friend and wondered where on Askí she was right now.

"There now." Mihko nodded at the children, then sat on the ground, followed quickly by Nicky and Ochek, who sat on either side of the fire, on the benches. He motioned to the benches, an invitation for the children to sit there as well. Morgan hurried to sit beside Ochek, wanting to stay next to him, and Eli sat beside Nicky. When they'd taken their places around the fire, Mihko continued. "Now that we've been introduced to one another, maybe you'd like to tell me how you came through the Great Tree. I've always been curious about *that* . . . gateway."

"We call it a portal," Morgan said.

"Isn't that"—Ochek glanced at his father—"kind of the same thing?"

"I think so," Nicky said.

"*Semantics.*" Morgan physically waved the difference away as though shooing a fly. "Anyway, the portal, or gateway, or whatever. I'm just curious: Ochek didn't seem all that . . . amazed . . . that we'd come through it."

"Oh," Mihko said, "I wouldn't have been either."

"We know there are . . . portals . . . in the North Country, dear," Nicky said.

"I *told* you, humans had come here before," Ochek said.

"What other portals?" Morgan wondered if humans in other parts of the world, her world, had come to Askí before. "Where are they?"

"We believe most of them are in the northern woods, where—" But Mihko abruptly stopped.

"That's *so* annoying!" Ochek said. "It's not like if you say its name, it's going to appear out of nowhere and take our souls."

"Silence! You know we don't speak of it!" Mihko said.

"I think it's alright," Nicky said to her husband calmly. "Nobody's seen it for many seasons."

Fantasy creature talk! Morgan thought.

"Sooo many seasons," Ochek said.

"That doesn't matter," Mihko argued. "There's a reason why that is, and it's because we don't utter its name."

"I literally just told Morgan and Eli the story of Kihiw on the way over here, and I said its name, and I don't see it anywhere." He looked around the room to make his point, even checking under the benches. Mihko looked incredibly annoyed. Morgan didn't think that even she would be so audacious. "Nope." Ochek shrugged. "No giant."

"You'd best sleep with one eye open, boy," Mihko said.

"*It*," Nicky said, while Mihko fumed, "lives in the northern woods, and since we've vowed never to venture into those woods, nobody has seen it for many years. Too many years to count."

Unless you made notches in the wood, Morgan thought. "My brother's told me that Mista—" Morgan stopped herself from finishing the word. She didn't want to make Mihko angrier and risk outstaying their welcome when it had only just begun. "My brother's told me," she restarted, "that *it* can open portals. That it can go from one dimension to another. Yours and ours."

"That's true," Mihko said. "It opens the portals. We aren't sure how, but we've never been able to ask."

"It isn't the talkative sort," Ochek said, "being that it's *never around*."

"But if *you* let us know how you came from the portal," Nicky prompted.

"And about your world," Ochek said.

"Do you"—Mihko looked at them both carefully, inquisitively—"have magical powers?"

"I mean, my brother might, but I don't. We just . . ." Morgan thought about how to explain it so that it wouldn't sound so far-fetched, but that was pretty much impossible. "Well, I doubt the giant does the same thing, unless it keeps a drawing pad and pencil crayons handy in its, like, cave home or whatever."

"I don't have powers. I can just draw," Eli said.

"Yeah. So, Eli drew a picture, from the perspective of the Great Tree, of the Barren Grounds, and we placed it on a wall in the attic of our house and it opened like a window into exactly what Eli drew."

"What's an attic?" Ochek asked.

"Yes, is that a special room for magic?" Mihko asked.

"No," Morgan said. "No, an attic is just a regular room at the top of a house, below the roof."

"So we are in an attic right now, then," Mihko said, motioning to the roof.

"How do I . . ." Morgan racked her brain. "Yes, it's under a roof, but an attic is at the top of a house, and really it's just the space between the roof and an actual room that people live in. Most of the time." She tried to assess whether the fishers understood her.

Mihko looked thoughtful. He stared into the fire, then

looked up. "You're right, I doubt the giant uses . . . pencil crayons and a drawing pad to open portals."

"It *could* draw something on the things it makes into portals, like the drawings we have on the Council Hut walls," Ochek offered. "It would just need ocher."

Morgan wondered if Ochek was right, and if so, could the portal in the Great Tree open to other places on earth? She and Eli had never tried, but maybe the giant was able to go wherever it wanted from whatever portal existed in the North Country. And did that mean if the children decided to try, if Eli drew a picture on Askí and placed it on the Great Tree, they, too, could go to another place on earth? Or even to another time? The thought excited Morgan. She could go forward in time, check out scores in big sports games, or lottery numbers, then go back to the present day and be a millionaire! She decided that one day they would test that theory.

"Uhhh, Morgan?" Eli waved a hand in front of her face. "Hello?"

"Oh right. Sorry." Morgan gave her head a shake. Back to reality.

"She does that," Eli told the family of fishers.

"I *do* daydream, and *my brother* has a tendency to point out all my eccentricities and it's super annoying."

"Sorry," Eli said in a tone that made Morgan think he wasn't actually very sorry.

Morgan felt ashamed. Not because she'd daydreamed or because Eli had pointed out the fact that she did. She was used to getting lost in her thoughts, and she was used to Eli getting after her about things she did. It was because thinking about traveling to the future just to get rich felt like a very Mason thing. She vowed, in that moment, not to think about things like that again. It felt much better, no matter how much it hurt, to daydream about her mother.

"No need to apologize, Morgan," Mihko said. "But tell me . . ." He turned his attention to Eli. "How did you know to draw this place if you'd never seen it before? Surely *that* is magic."

"I don't know what it is," Eli said. "All I can say is that I didn't even think about drawing this place. I just saw it. Like, in my head."

Morgan expected the animal beings, all three of them, to look confused. As bewildered as she felt when she thought about it. How could he *just know* to draw this place? Morgan had wondered that often. How was it even possible? Did he manifest Askí, Misewa, Ochek, all of it, out of nothing? Did he summon this place into existence? Did he create an entire history? No. Eli wasn't a god. He didn't create life just by touching a pencil to paper. Writers created worlds and people and histories and conflicts from their imaginations, but those worlds didn't become real. They just *felt* real to readers. Eli had drawn a place that already existed and, somehow, they'd journeyed there. Somehow, he was connected to it enough to draw it, to open a portal to it. They belonged here. She'd known that for a long while. They needed to be here. Maybe, she considered, this place needed them as well.

Mihko nodded knowingly. He didn't look confused at all. "This place," he said deliberately, "is woven into the fabric of your beings. It's a part of you, and it always has been. Kayas, long ago. Before time was. It called you here for whatever reason, and you heard its call. When you know a place in this way, when you know it before you've seen it, it's called blood memory. That's why you are welcome to stay here. That's why you *must* stay here. Will you stay, little ones?"

Eli nodded.

Morgan spoke without thinking about it for even a split second. She didn't notice the word come out of her mouth. It felt like the first time they'd been here. It felt as though they'd always been here. It felt like they would always be here.

"Ehe."

FOURTEEN

The siblings slept on the floor in the fisher family's longhouse that night, after being fed supper and spending the rest of the evening talking about life in the North Country and the history of the village. Morgan and Eli had been told these stories before, but they both acted as though it was the first time. In turn, Morgan and Eli told the animal beings about their lives. Eli talked about the home he still remembered. He talked about living on the land with his grandfather. He talked about being raised traditionally, and how, because of that, Misewa already felt like home to him. When the animal beings heard about Eli's experience on the land, Mihko offered, when he felt it was time, to take the children onto his trapline.

"But the journey is arduous, little ones," he warned.

Morgan and Eli worked hard to keep straight faces, because they had been to the trapline, and under the *most* arduous conditions.

Morgan shared her own story as well, though she felt it was far less interesting. She didn't remember much about her home. The clearest memory was always of her mother holding her as a toddler, in a rocking chair in the corner of a small room. The knocking came against the front door of the house, then the footsteps, then the darkness, and Morgan was taken away. She may have been out on the land as a baby but she couldn't remember. Her story was of the homes she'd lived in over the course of her short life, the awful things she'd lived through, and how lucky she and Eli were to have the foster parents they had now. It was the first time Morgan had felt that her foster parents could, one day, be like real parents. How strange to feel that way, with Katie and James a world away. But there it was.

"You know," she said, more to herself but speaking out loud regardless, "they mess up, but I think all parents mess up. In small ways or in big ways. The difference between Katie and James and my other foster parents is that when they mess up, they're doing it with a good heart. They actually care about me and Eli." She paused, and looked down at the moccasins they'd given her. She wiggled her toes around inside of them. "They're not so bad. They're not my real parents, but . . ."

"You know," Nicky said, "Níwakomakanak, my relatives, are all the beings in this village, whether they are blood or not. It's the same for you."

After that first night, Mihko and Ochek helped set up a teepee outside of their longhouse for the children to stay in while they were in Misewa. It was during the construction of the teepee that they were told about the other teepees in the village.

Misewa was a gathering place. It was where other animal beings came, and stayed for a short while, following the movements of the four-legged ones and the fish. This was how many of the animal beings on this world subsisted. If they were hungry, they followed the food source, moving from place to place at different times of the year. When the seasons changed and the food was scarce in one area, the visitors would move on. The animal beings who stayed in Misewa permanently were able to do so because of hunters like Mihko, who had traplines all over the southern woods. Any beings were welcome to stay in the village, with Council's approval, but most preferred a nomadic life, living on the land rather than in a longhouse.

"What about the wigwam things in the trees?" Morgan asked during the construction of their teepee. "Who lives in those?"

"The birds," Ochek said. "Seven warriors who have watched over this place for the last few seasons. They, like others, came here to visit, and chose to stay."

The Bird Warriors were rarely seen. Even several days after Morgan and Eli had settled into the village, neither one of them had managed to get a clear look at those that lived in the trees. From time to time, they would burst out of their dwellings and soar into the air, over the southern woods, in search of food and on the lookout for predators.

"Predators like who?" Eli asked, perhaps too eagerly.

Morgan knew that he was thinking of Mahihkan. A predator who became a protector.

"There are many beings that stalk these woods and this place," Mihko said. "There is, of course, the giant of the northern woods. Though nobody has seen it for many years, we're still wary."

"Obviously, since you won't even say its name," Ochek said.

"Wolves come down from the mountains and search for food out in the woods, and every few seasons, unpredictably, the Great Bear comes through the North Country and terrorizes its villages."

Eli and Morgan traded a look, and Morgan mouthed, "Muskwa?" to Eli, who shook his head as if to say, *No way.*

Morgan agreed, but had a nagging feeling that was hard to shake. Muskwa was, even in his old age, considered a Great Bear, but it seemed impossible to think of him as an animal being who would terrorize other villages. There simply must have been another Great Bear in the North Country. The only thing she knew for sure was that, at this time, Muskwa had not yet arrived in the village and so was not yet Chief of Misewa. She knew this because Wapistan (which meant "marten," Eli told her) was currently Chief of Misewa. Wapistan was one of the oldest and wisest of the animal beings gathered in the village at the northern edge of the woods overlooking the Barren Grounds.

Many of the villagers came to welcome the children on their first night in the teepee, after news of their presence had spread throughout Misewa. They remembered how they'd been greeted on their first visit—the beaver slapping its tail, the caribou throwing a snowball, the bison shaking its head, the bewilderment at their presence, the anger, the resentment. This time around, those same animal beings, the ones they had come to know and love and consider family, brought the children gifts and food, each one of them welcoming the siblings with warmth and kindness. And as each one entered their teepee, Morgan and Eli had to pretend that they had never met them before, and were careful not to show the sort of affection that they had towards them.

The next night, Chief Wapistan and Council came to see the new visitors. The Council members were the same: Oho, the owl, and Miskinahk, the turtle. It was only the Chief that was different. After Oho and Miskinahk had entered the teepee and sat down across from Morgan and Eli, Chief Wapistan, with a crooked but sturdy cane, struggled into the dwelling, moving as slowly and deliberately, Morgan thought, as Yoda. A great silence fell as soon as the Chief of Misewa had opened the flap and made his way towards the fire. The silence continued as Wapistan sat down with assistance from his two Council members. He wore a forest green cloak with a hood that cast shadows over his face. In the same slow and deliberate manner in which he'd walked into the teepee, he pulled the hood off and locked eyes with Morgan and Eli.

"Tansi, young ones," Chief Wapistan said.

"Tansi," said both the siblings.

His voice was soft, like clouds whispering, but carried clearly over the crackling and snapping of the fire and into Morgan's ears. It felt as if he were communicating with them telepathically, only moving his mouth for show.

"I know that Mihko, in his kindness, has invited you both to stay here in Misewa. However, he knows, as well as any being in this place, that that decision belongs to us."

The Chief looked to Oho, then to Miskinahk. This was the way Morgan knew it had to be. Any decision of importance rested with the community's leadership.

"Ehe, Chief," Eli said.

"Yes," Morgan agreed. "Ehe, totally."

Wapistan reached for his cane, which was a smooth branch, and placed it across his lap. He placed a hand on either end, and looked at it from the handle to the tip, which was worn dull from supporting the aging being. He raised his head, and regarded the siblings with eyes that were as black as Ochek's.

"When Amisk chews at the trunk of a tree, the tree falls. The trunk is broken, and in its brokenness, it reveals itself. The tree does the same when it's chopped down to provide for us. Our houses, our meat racks"—the Chief patted the handle of his cane—"a walking stick for an old marten like me. What it reveals, children, are its rings. Those rings share with others the time it has lived on Askí. The Great Tree across the Barren Grounds, if it were ever to fall, would have so many rings they would be hard to count. It's been here for far more years than me. A young tree, small and prone to bend in a strong wind, a sapling, has very few rings. If it survives, if it grows strong despite its struggles, despite the obstacles it faces, its rings will grow outward like ripples in water."

Wapistan breathed deeply, and Morgan heard his breath shake like a rattle. Whatever the Chief's age, she feared that his time was short. She knew that he wouldn't survive the White Time, but she worried that he wouldn't even survive the time she hoped he would allow them to stay.

Wapistan nodded his head, and the intensity of his gaze turned soft, like his voice.

"When I first saw you and your brother," he said directly to Morgan, "I thought you were both saplings." He spoke again, to both of them now. "That is to say, I thought you had very few rings in your trunks, that you had faced, if anything in your young lives, a calm breeze, not a strong wind. I thought you couldn't have yet experienced many struggles." He grasped his walking stick as if for support, even though he was sitting securely on the ground. "We can make quick judgments, even the wisest of us." He started to laugh, then coughed instead. "They tell me I'm wise anyway. Sometimes I feel like a sapling trapped in this old body."

Miskinahk looked to be holding back tears. Oho placed their feather-fingers on Wapistan's shoulder. The Chief continued.

"I was wrong about you, Morgan and Eli. Struggled you have."

He even talks like Yoda! Morgan thought excitedly. *And Eli will* never *get that reference until he actually watches* Empire*!*

"You have faced strong winds and brutal elements in your lives. You have, even though you are, most certainly, just saplings. Something has made you strong. Stronger than even you think you are."

Eli looked to be fighting back tears, for a reason different than Miskinahk's. Eli pulled off his hood, as Wapistan had, and ran his fingers across his shortened strands of hair. She knew that he didn't feel strong. She didn't either.

"And while I don't recognize you, I see recognition in your eyes. Maybe you've lived the way we do, before, on your world, or maybe"—another pause, another shaky breath—"or maybe there's something else."

Morgan felt breathless and speechless. How could he know? What did he know? Did blood memory work backward? Did the time they'd spent on Misewa in the future somehow reach back and tell Wapistan something about them?

"Whatever the case, I see that you have come here in a good way, with good intentions. I don't think you would do anything to harm the beings here in Misewa, and because of that, I agree with Mihko. You are welcome to stay here with us for as long as you like." Chief Wapistan lifted his cane, grasped the handle with his paw, and pressed the end into the ground. With help from Oho and Miskinahk, he rose to his feet. So much about him looked like Ochek, the type of animal he was. Eli would know more about that, but a marten seemed a lot like a fisher.

With Wapistan's free paw, he replaced his hood, and shadows painted his face with darkness. "Níwakomakanak, my relatives, sleep well tonight."

"Ekosani, Chief," Morgan said.

"Ekosani," Eli said.

After they had been officially welcomed to stay, Morgan and Eli eased into life in the Misewa of the past. Morgan made sure, however, to keep track of the days; she always kept count, so that she knew when she and Eli had to leave for earth. In those first few days, Morgan couldn't help worrying about what was going on back home. This time was different, as they had left during the day, which meant that Katie and James were not sleeping. She tried to put it out of her mind that Katie could call her at any moment from work to check on how she and Eli were doing. Or, worse yet, Katie could come home to check on them over the lunch hour (Morgan didn't have to worry about this possibility for three weeks or so in Misewa time). As the days passed by, however, this worry abated. Every new day brought the rising sun, and with it, less anxiety.

And it was hard to feel worry or nervousness or sadness or any negative emotion where they were. Morgan and Eli were living the good life in Misewa, and all of those bad feelings were forgotten, especially when they were with Ochek, with whom they spent most of their time. They enjoyed seeing him as a teenager, displaying an immaturity that he'd never shown as an adult. When he stormed out of the house, or threw himself onto his hide blanket, when Nicky or Mihko did or said something he didn't like. When he talked back to his parents in the same way that Morgan did. When he snuck off in the night to do something he wasn't allowed to do by himself during the day. But soon even these differences fell away, just like their worry, and it didn't matter that he'd become more of a friend than a mentor. Ochek was Ochek, and nothing else mattered.

The days turned into weeks, and the children became more and more a part of the village. The villagers appreciated the siblings and their willingness, their eagerness, to live in a good way. They were helpful, and were always sure never to take more than what was given to them, to always respect the land they were living on and the beings—four-legged and two-legged—on it. There came a time, too, when Morgan didn't think much about her inability to call her birth mother, and she didn't think Eli thought much about the bullies who had terrorized him. He was a different kid in Misewa; he always had been. On earth, he was quiet and withdrawn. Here, Eli was happy, confident, and, Morgan dared to say, carefree.

The truth was, so was she.

FIFTEEN

Very early one morning, with the sky still a midnight blue and the sun yet to rise, Morgan was stirred awake by the flap of their teepee opening. Though their first night in the teepee had seen an endless procession of visitors, after four weeks, the siblings were no longer a novelty, so Morgan was a bit startled. Who could this be? She propped herself up on one elbow, blinked her eyes awake, and rubbed her face. Slowly, Mihko came into focus, and standing behind him was Ochek.

"Good morning, children," Mihko said.

"Hey, Eli." Morgan reached across the extinguished firepit to shove her brother and wake him up. "Pssst."

Eli moaned, turned over onto his back, rubbed his eyes, and, finally, opened them. "What is it?" he said in a gravelly, not-yet-awake voice. He looked at Morgan first, but when she nodded towards the entrance of the teepee, he saw the animal beings. At the sight of them, he sat up quickly.

Morgan sat up as well, and peered around Mihko and

Ochek to get a sense of the time. She noticed the darkness. "What's going on?"

"Last night," Mihko said, "I told my son that I thought it was time. I asked if you were ready, and he said that you are. So, I'd like it if both of you came with us to the trapline."

Morgan felt excitement rise in her chest. She was beaming. Eli was too. They'd been waiting for this moment.

"I should warn you," Ochek said, "it's a *long* walk through the southern woods. Especially for humans."

"Don't worry about us," she said. "I'm pretty sure *these* humans can handle it."

Mihko, who had been holding an armful of leather clothing, presented it then to the humans. "Nicky made these for you," he said as the siblings began to sift through the selection: two pairs of pants—tan colored, with sinew already woven through the belt loops—and two tops. "You've been walking around in your earth clothing since arriving in Misewa, and she thought it was time you wore something else."

Eli took out a long-sleeved black top with a forest green pouch and hood. He held it up and inspected it, delighted.

"Nimama thought you might like that one," Ochek pointed out. "You walk around with that hood over your hair all the time."

Morgan would have let Eli have the hooded top even if she'd picked first. What she was left with looked like a long-sleeved Henley shirt, only it was stained red with ocher, and instead of plastic buttons, there were tiny bones. Morgan was pleased with the top. She thought it looked like something she'd wear to school on earth. It was soft, and she was sure it would be comfortable.

"Ekosani," she said. "These are beautiful."

"Ekosani," Eli said.

"Nicky will be pleased you like them," Mihko said.

"You should get dressed quickly," Ochek told them. "We came to eat breakfast with you so that we can head out before the sun comes up."

They had berries, fish, bannock, and sweet tea for breakfast, and the food was fresh and bursting with flavor, the way food straight from the land tastes. Mihko explained to the children that they'd need to fill up for the journey, that they wouldn't stop until lunch, when the sun was at its highest point in the sky. After breakfast, they packed what they'd need—materials for the tent, preserves to eat until they could catch and pick food, extra clothing, tools—and left Misewa, each with a pack on their shoulders.

The sun had yet to rise, and the midnight blue of the sky had only just started to shift to a lighter shade. All the other villagers were still asleep; there were no lights behind shuttered windows, no smoke rising from longhouses and teepees. Only when Morgan looked up into the trees did she see a sign of life: one of the seven birds that lived in the wigwams high above.

Just like Tahtakiw the crane, who'd fled Misewa with Mason after the human had stolen the summer birds, and Oho the owl, these birds looked almost exactly like any other bird she might have seen flying around back in Winnipeg, on earth. But the protector bird was much bigger, maybe two or three feet high. And their feathery fingers were more functional. This bird had one wing tip wrapped tightly around a sharpened staff, a particularly dangerous-looking weapon. Not as dangerous-looking, though, as the sword strapped to their back. Their white breast was puffed out and burned bright in the dim light of the breaking day. If they noticed Morgan, they gave no indication. But she couldn't take her eyes off them, as surely as they could not take their eyes off the Barren Grounds, scanning all the way to the west and all the way to the east. Keeping watch diligently.

Morgan, close enough to Mihko, tapped him on the shoulder.

"What is it, Morgan?" Mihko asked quietly, not wanting to wake any villagers.

Morgan pointed at the bird outside of the wigwam, perched on a thick branch, staring off across the land that surrounded the village. Mihko nodded, then looked away, as though even looking at the bird would disturb their duty.

"That is Pip."

"Pip?" Morgan repeated. "Really?"

"I wouldn't make fun of *anything* to do with Pip," Ochek said. "Especially not his name."

"No, I'm not, it's just"—Morgan tried to think of the right thing to say—"that's such a fantasy creature name. If I were writing a fantasy story, I'd totally name a character Pip."

"I think it might just be short for something else," Eli said. "Pipisché?"

"Ehe," Ochek said. "Robin."

"Robin?" Morgan took another look at the bird, who was just barely still in view. "But shouldn't he have a red breast, then? His breast is white."

"We both know not everything is the same here," Eli said. "Robins just might have a white breast."

"Good point," Morgan conceded. "Robins are also not, like, a couple of feet high on earth."

"Exactly."

"Pip is the leader of the seven Bird Warriors who watch over this place," Mihko said.

"And you said they've been here for a few seasons?" Eli asked.

"That's right."

"Where were they before they settled in Misewa?" Morgan asked. "Just flying around and stuff?"

"Nobody knows," Ochek said. "Or if they do, nobody has said. But the birds are very old, and very dangerous."

"A good group to have on your side," Mihko said, "but not the best company."

"I just like to know they're up there," Ochek said.

Morgan looked once more at Pip, who was still standing at attention. Then, as though sensing her gaze, he locked eyes with her, his head darting quickly in her direction. It startled Morgan enough that she tripped over a tree root and fell. Eli helped her up, and when she recovered, she found that Pip was gone. He'd either gone back into his wigwam or flown off.

"He disappeared, just like Batman," Morgan said in awe.

"I told you, he's a robin, not a bat," Ochek said.

A discussion about superheroes followed as the quartet left Misewa to begin their expedition.

The journey to Mihko's trapline took them southeast through the woods. Ochek and Mihko were leading the way, and Morgan and Eli trailed behind. The siblings had been this way countless times, and if they hadn't known they were in the past, they would never have suspected it. Nothing was different, no matter how far they went. Not the trees, not the undergrowth, not the streams that offered clean water to quench their thirst, not the roots revealing themselves from underneath the ground, and not the subtle path that promised to lead them exactly where they intended to go.

At midday, the group stopped. They were approaching the canyon.

Morgan found herself staring at Ochek, so it was a good thing his back was turned to her—he might have found her gaze a bit creepy. She still couldn't believe that he was alive, even after the last few weeks they'd spent in Misewa. Walking through the southern woods the way they used to, it had hit her again. He was *alive.* But as soon as they left, he wouldn't be. One day soon, they would have to leave, and it would feel like they were killing him. Her only consolation was that they could always come back to this time and place if they wanted to see him. In fact, what was stopping them from making this past time their regular destination?

Why not come back to *right now* and stay for several weeks every time they wanted to visit?

They decided to stop for lunch, and while the fishers prepared the food, Morgan and Eli went looking for the items necessary to build a spit for cooking. With a rare moment alone together when they couldn't be overheard, Morgan suggested to Eli, "What if we just came back *here* all the time?"

"And just become professional time travelers?"

"He doesn't have to be dead." Morgan broke off a twig from a tree and flicked her thumb against the green threads that had connected it to its source of life.

Eli took the twig from Morgan, and dropped it on the ground. "But he *is* dead, Morgan."

"Is he?" Morgan picked up the same twig, and used it to point at Ochek. The animal being was busily cutting meat to cook. "He looks pretty alive to me."

"*Was* alive, and you know that." Eli tried to take the twig again but Morgan snatched it away. He shook his head. "Someday, a man's going to come here. He'll take the summer birds. The White Time will be here for a long time. Then we'll find Askí, and Ochek is going to—"

"I know the story, Eli. I was there too."

"So you know that he has to die in order to save the North Country and Misewa."

"Not if . . ." Morgan scrambled through a hundred thoughts, pacing back and forth and waving the stick like a music conductor. "Not if we go back to . . . to the first time we came here and"—she stopped and turned towards Eli, wide-eyed—"do things differently. We know where the summer birds will be. We know what Mason will do to try and stop us. We could prepare better, we could—"

"Are you listening to yourself?! We made the rules *really* simple, Morgan. We can't tell them what's going to happen."

"I just . . ." Morgan's lower lip began to quiver. She tried to choke back tears. It didn't work.

"We can keep coming back here, I guess," Eli said, "but what about the villagers in *our* time? We'll miss them, and they'll miss us. And the more we come back here"—Eli stepped closer to Morgan—"we're just going to keep missing Ochek worse than we already do. I think when we leave here, we shouldn't come back."

"No." Morgan could barely whisper the word.

"Yes." Eli put his arms around his sister and hugged her.

Morgan unwrapped her own arms, which had been held tight around her body, and put them around her brother. They blended into a hunk of crying humans, Eli's head resting on her shoulder, her head resting on top of his, their arms grasping each other tightly. They stayed like that until Ochek called out, "Hey! What're you guys doing? The meat's ready!"

"Coming!" Morgan called back to Ochek.

Her face was still pressed against Eli's hair, because his hood had fallen down on account of the hug. She raised her head and leaned away from her brother. He looked different. In his eyes, his face. She picked up strands of his hair that had been tied back into a high ponytail, the only type of ponytail the length of his hair would allow. But it had grown. It was inches longer than when they'd arrived in Misewa. Ochek had been putting fish oil in it. One day, he'd asked why Eli always wore his hood up, and Eli told him what had happened and why he'd cut it. The animal being said the oil would work to help his hair grow faster.

"When did you get so old, huh?" she asked her brother. "How'd you get so much smarter than me?"

Morgan looked at the twig. It was perfect for a spit. They started on the short walk back to the spot that had been picked out for lunch.

"I don't want to leave either," Eli said.

"I know," Morgan said.

"It's just . . ."

"Yeah. I know. Let's just enjoy the time we have with him." Morgan stared at Ochek again, and this time he was looking at her. She smiled. He smiled back. "People usually don't get these kinds of goodbyes."

"I guess we're lucky."

"Yeah. I guess we are."

They ate a meal of berries they had picked along the way, as well as wapos meat cooked over the fire, and tea Mihko made. It was delicious, and though the hike through the woods was tiring, the lunch refreshed their energy. They ate like characters on *The Simpsons* for the first while, shoveling food into their mouths without much time between bites to breathe, let alone talk. But then the topic of names came into Morgan's head, something she'd always been obsessed with, and she decided to break the silence, despite having a mouthful of rabbit.

"Hey." She continued to chew, and eventually swallowed. "Know how all the animal beings in the North Country have names that are just what they actually are?" The question was rhetorical so nobody answered her. "But"—she put up a finger, asking them to wait while she swallowed—"you're"—she pointed at Mihko—"a fisher too, and *not* named Ochek, and Ochek's mom is also a fisher, and she's not named Ochek either. Why are you not named after the thing you are *and* what do your names mean?"

"I know what Mihko—" Eli began.

"*Thanks*, Eli," Morgan said, interrupting. "Maybe . . . okay, let me rephrase. What do your names mean, and why are you called what you're called?"

"You're going to have to figure out how to answer that, Nipapa." Ochek laughed.

Mihko laughed too. "I'll give it a try." He swallowed the food he'd been chewing. "First off, it would be confusing if we were all named Ochek, wouldn't it?"

"Right?" Morgan said. "That's what I've been saying."

"My wife, Nicky, as she told you children, her full name is Nikamon, which means 'a song.' Of course, all names come from somewhere. There was a time when our children would be named for things that happened during their birth."

"Like what?" Morgan asked.

"Okay, well . . . let's say that a child is born, and right after, a storm rolls in and there is so much thunder that it sounds like drumming from Creator's hands. The parents might name that child Pinésíwan, which means 'it is thundering.'"

"That sounds a bit more inventive than, you know, you're a cat, so we're going to name you Cat."

"Pos," Eli said.

"Yeah, see? Nobody wants to be named Pos."

"What's the story behind Nikamon?" Eli asked.

"When my wife was a baby, just a small little fisher, her mother used to rock her in her arms, just like this." Mihko ghosted the motion, like a slow dance, of a mother rocking her child. "While she rocked her baby, the mother—"

"Hummed a song." Morgan was suddenly lost in her own memory of being a toddler, rocked in her mother's arms, and being sung to. Her heart began to beat hard in time with the song she remembered. *Thump, thump, thump, thump, thump, thump, thump.*

"Yes, that's right," Mihko said.

"What song did she hum? Do you know it?" Morgan asked desperately, like if she heard the song Nicky's mother had hummed, it would somehow bring her closer to her own mother. Jenny Trout.

"That's something you'll have to ask Nicky," Mihko said. "It's not my song. But it's one that she hummed to herself all the time when she was a child. So much so that one day, her parents decided to name her Nikamon, 'a song,' because of the song she loved so much."

"I like that story," Morgan said.

"Just wait until you hear it a million times," Ochek said.

"Excuse my son," Mihko said. "In his youth he sometimes forgets his manners. He'll grow out of it."

"What about you?" Eli asked. "Where does Mihko come from? It means—"

"'Blood.'" Mihko's face turned grave, and he, like Morgan, became lost in thought, remembering a time that had long passed. She knew the look. It was a long time before he said, "There is a story about how I came to be called Mihko. My name used to be Ochek. That's why my son carries that name. But I . . ." He stared deep into the heart of the fire. "That story is for another—"

Crack.

The sound came like a snapping bone, jolting Mihko and everybody else into silence. Ochek raised a finger to his lips. The siblings nodded their agreement. Ochek looked as though he knew exactly what had made that sound. Mihko didn't seem to have a doubt either; he busily kicked dirt over the fire, snuffing it out, and most importantly killing the smoke. And as soon as the fire was out completely, he grabbed what was left of their lunch and, acting very animal-like, furiously dug a hole, tossed the meat into it, and then covered it up to conceal the smell.

Crack.

The sound was closer this time, like a thunderstorm approaching. Only it was no storm. The skies were clear in all directions for as far as Morgan could see. And thunderstorms, as far as she knew, did not cause the ground to tremble as though the earth itself was afraid, like the two fishers.

Mihko raised his paw towards the other three, motioning for them to stay where they were. With great stealth, he moved forward through the woods, towards the sound. Curious but careful, the other three inched ahead until they were at the edge of the small clearing, just far enough to be able to see Mihko. He was on all fours and navigating his way deeper and deeper into the forest. Every time another sound came, drawing ever closer, he would stop for a moment, and then continue on. Until suddenly he stopped behind a large tree, and peered out around it.

The ground shook again, and again, and soon enough it was shaking every second, rhythmically. Off to their left, southeast from where they knelt at the edge of the clearing, bushes began to shake. It wasn't long before the source of the cracking, the trembling, the shaking, revealed itself. A bear crashed through the brush just a few feet away from where the children hid with Ochek. It stalked along the ground, each great big paw causing the ground to shake anew. By the size of it, Morgan realized that this was not just any bear; it was, in fact, the Great Bear Mihko had spoken about.

Mihko had his back against the large tree, hiding as best he could from the beast. Eli and Ochek were on their knees, peering out from behind the cover of bushes, making sure the bear couldn't see them. Morgan ran behind a tree, and watched the predator through the foliage. In her haste, she'd made a rustling noise—her clothes against the bark. The bear stopped for a second, and seemed to stare straight at her. Morgan could scarcely breathe, for in that moment, when she saw its eyes, she knew it was Muskwa.

SIXTEEN

Morgan no longer felt any fear. He may have looked huge and fierce, but this was the bear she'd spent months living with in the same village. The bear that she had eaten with. The one she had rested her head against while looking at the stars. And there was little doubt in her mind that they were looking at Muskwa. He was walking on four legs, but it was unmistakable. He was wearing the same sort of clothing that he always did—forest green pants and a black vest. He was almost the same size, maybe a bit bigger, because he would shrink in his old age. He had the same face, the same eyes. Kind eyes, Morgan thought, even now, which made everybody else's fear confusing.

Mihko stayed where he was, ahead of the other three, keeping watch protectively, waiting until it was safe, until the Great Bear had passed, before daring to move again and return to the clearing. Eli and Ochek hadn't moved. They were still on their knees, looking in Muskwa's direction, craning their necks to see over the bushes. Her brother appeared confused, like Morgan, but also afraid, like Ochek and Mihko. Why? Eli knew Muskwa as well as Morgan did. Eli had lived with Misewa's Chief for as many days, had feasted with him, had talked with him, had gone for walks with him into the woods or out across the Barren Grounds. What was there to fear?

Morgan walked over to Ochek and Eli, not bothering to hide at all, now that she knew who the Great Bear was. The beast was looking in another direction and didn't see her.

"Are you crazy?" Ochek asked. "Do you want to get killed?"

"You're telling me that that bear right there"—Morgan pointed directly at Muskwa, who had now passed them by—"that big cuddly bear—"

"Cuddly?" Ochek said.

"—goes around terrorizing villages in the North Country?"

"Yes, that's what I'm telling you. He comes to the villages whenever he feels like it, takes whatever he wants, which is pretty much everything, and then leaves us to re-store our food, repair our longhouses, all of that."

"*That's* the Great Bear," Morgan said. "You're totally, 100 percent sure, without any doubt whatsoever."

"He just told you it was," Eli said.

"You know who that is, right, Eli?"

Eli gave Morgan a wide-eyed look, his head tilted to one side. It was to say to her, as she understood the gesture, that the fishers couldn't know that *they* knew the Great Bear was Muskwa.

"That's what I thought," Morgan whispered, just loud enough for Eli to hear.

"I'm totally, 100 percent sure," Ochek said. "It's really hard to forget who it is that destroys your home."

Mihko returned with the same quiet, precise movement. They were all kneeling at the edge of the clearing now, watching the bear, who was about twenty feet away, sauntering off to the west without a care in the world.

"At least he's not going in Misewa's direction," Mihko said.

"Yet," Ochek said.

"Ehe. Yet. Eventually, he'll make his way there."

"And then what?" Morgan asked.

"Some predators you fight," Ochek said. "Some, you choose your lives over food, houses, the village."

"Has anybody ever tried just talking to him? Like, ask him not to wreck everything and just, you know, offer him food or something?" Morgan asked.

"Whatever we'd offer wouldn't be enough for the Great Bear," Mihko said.

"Yeah, because we'd never offer him every single thing we have, which is what he wants," Ochek added.

An idea came to Morgan. An impulse, more accurately, that came from a hundred memories she had of her time with Muskwa. Conversations they'd had. He'd always been so easy to talk to. He'd always listened. She just couldn't reconcile *her* Muskwa with this apparently terrible bear, no matter how hard she tried. The Great Bear, as they called him, may not have known her yet, but she knew him. And people, animal beings, didn't change that much.

They weren't evil enough to destroy somebody's home and then, years later, gentle enough to allow a girl to lean against them, to feel comforted in a time of sadness. Morgan had had outbursts of anger many times, but that wasn't who she was. She always felt bad about doing things like slamming her hand against the dinner table or making her foster mother cry. She decided that even if Muskwa did the things they said he did, it wasn't really him. If it was, he wouldn't be the bear she had come to know and love, and to hold in her heart as family. She started off towards him. He was still in sight, still walking westward, still doing so at a relaxed pace, unaware of the group's presence.

"What are you doing, child?" Mihko whispered sharply.

"Maybe the right person hasn't talked to him yet," Morgan said. "If you've bothered to talk to him at all."

"And you are? A human from another world who he doesn't even know?" Ochek said.

"I think I can talk some sense into him, yeah," Morgan said. "I don't think he's really like that."

"I've seen it," Mihko said, "and trust me, he's really like that. We should judge others by their actions, and the bear's actions tell another story. I can't let you risk your life because you're naive."

"Morgan . . . ," Eli started.

"You've got to understand what I'm saying, right? At least you," Morgan said. "I know you understand."

Eli paused. "I think they're right. We don't know *this* bear. I don't know if he's the bear you *think* he can be . . . right now. Something might happen that will change how he is, but you can't just go over there hoping for that."

"Yes, I can, because maybe *this* is that something." Morgan scanned the faces of the group she'd traveled this far with. They were all looking at her with pleading eyes, asking her not to go, but she'd already made up her mind. They could look at her with puppy-dog eyes as big as Eli's, and she wouldn't stop. "I can and I will." She nodded confidently at the trio, then turned from them and walked away. Muskwa was easy to follow. The cracking branches. The trembling ground. The shaking bushes.

She wasn't long into her pursuit of him before she felt a hand on her shoulder. It was Eli.

"You're supposed to be on my side, you know," Morgan said.

"I *am* on your side, but—"

"See, when you say 'but' after agreeing with me, you're not really agreeing with me. Then again, you never do."

"What are you talking about?"

"What am I . . ." Morgan groaned in frustration. "You're always nudging me or giving me a look or scolding me for doing something I'm not supposed to do."

"I'm just looking out for you," Eli pleaded.

"Aren't I the older one?" Morgan asked. "I'm supposed to be looking out for you, aren't I?"

Without expecting to, without wanting to, Morgan felt like crying. She wasn't sure what Eli saw in her right then, but she found her mind darting back to the sidewalk in front of the school, to the bullies who had stolen his drawing pad.

"I'm sorry," he finally said after long moments of silence, "you're right. Maybe I do that too much."

Morgan heard the bear moving farther and farther away. "Thanks. Now, I've got a bear to catch."

She started back in the direction of Muskwa, but stopped again when Eli said, "Wait."

"What?" she snapped.

"I just don't think this is one of those times where I'm doing *that* . . . too much. You don't know who Muskwa is right now."

"Yeah, I do."

"No, you don't. You can't. You meet him years from now, when he's a changed bear."

"People don't change that much, Eli. People are who they are. There's something inside of him that's good, and I know I can bring it out of him. Don't you trust me?"

Eli paused. He paused for too long. "I . . ."

"*Great*," Morgan said. "I get it. But you should get something too, Eli." She took a breath. "We don't ignore family. We don't let family just pass by. Níwakomakanak. My relatives. Always."

"He could kill you," Eli whispered, so quietly that Morgan could barely hear the words. But she did, and she brushed them off instantly.

"Brother," she said, and this time she put a hand on his shoulder, "he's not going to kill me."

"How do you—?"

"Because this is the past. We were already here, however many years ago this is. Right? I can't die in the past if I'm alive in the future."

"Are you serious?" Eli shouted, and then he covered his mouth, quickly realizing how loud he'd been.

Morgan had had enough. She started to jog in the

direction of Muskwa, and decided that nothing would stop her this time. "I'll be back after I save the day."

"How do you think Mason is dead but he's still going to show up here one day. Huh? You can—"

"We promised not to try and dissect time travel, remember?" she said, without breaking stride.

"Please!"

By this time, Morgan had gone too far to hear Eli clearly. And even if she could have, her mind was occupied with Muskwa and only Muskwa. Yes, she believed that he was inherently good, and that whatever he'd done to villages in the North Country wasn't who he really was, but even still, she had to figure out how to get through to him. How to speak to the *good* Great Bear, not the awful one who would steal food and destroy houses. Maybe it was simple. She just needed to be herself. And maybe, just as Wapistan had seemed to recognize something in the children, something that stretched back from the future to the past, Muskwa would recognize something in her as well. A vision, or even a feeling, of her sitting with him in the Barren Grounds, staring at the stars. How could she feel so safe with him then and there if she was not safe with him here and now?

Morgan kept jogging, navigating her way over thick roots and brush, across unsteady footing, and came closer and closer to Muskwa. When she had finally pulled ahead of him, she made a beeline and ran right out in front of the Great Bear. He was pulling berries off a bush, but as soon as she stopped, mere feet away from him, he turned his attention to her. When their eyes met, it was the first time she felt unsure of herself. But she swallowed whatever fear had bubbled to the surface and waved, awkwardly. *All that thinking about what to do and you wave?* she scolded herself.

"Hey," she said. "Muskwa, right?"

He took a thunderous step towards her, one that seemed intended to scare her away. But she stubbornly didn't move.

"Look, uhhh, you don't know me, I don't think, but I know that you don't want to keep ruining villages and taking all their food and stuff. You're better than that."

There was a moment of stillness. A moment where Morgan saw something in his eyes that hinted at what she thought she knew. That there was good in him begging to get out. That there was something in her that he knew, somewhere deep in his heart. But then, that look was gone. The Great Bear rose to stand on his hind legs and roared so loudly the ancient trees shook, and birds flew from their perches, and deer sprinted off in all directions. Morgan cupped her ears, but her eardrums still felt as if they might burst.

"I am better than all! Now move!" the bear said in what sounded almost exactly like his roar.

"Morgan!" Eli skidded to a stop near the face-off between Morgan and Muskwa.

The bear towered over her. He was twice her height, ten times her weight.

He roared.

"Eli?" All of Morgan's confidence had turned to fear. She wanted to scream, but her voice was almost gone. She wanted to run, but couldn't move. "Help me, please. I'm sorry. I'm so sorry."

She saw out of the corner of her eye that Eli was frozen

too. That he couldn't move. That he couldn't speak anymore. But she heard his voice in her mind.

He could kill you.

Muskwa landed on all fours, jolting the ground like an earthquake. He raised his arm, about to swat her out of the way as if she were nothing.

But before he could, Ochek and Mihko came flying through the air and landed on the Great Bear's back. He rose, once more, to his feet, and Mihko and Ochek hung on for dear life; Mihko's arms were wrapped around the bear's neck, and Ochek's arms circled around the bear's shoulder. Muskwa twisted violently to shake the fishers off. He struck down on their little arms to make them lose their grip. But they wouldn't relent.

Mihko managed to get himself up onto the bear's shoulders so that he was straddling his head, and started pounding down on Muskwa's face. The Great Bear reached up, grabbed the hunter by the scruff of his neck, and tossed him into the woods. Morgan watched as he tumbled across the ground. Ochek was kneeing the side of Muskwa's body, one hit after another, and the bear grabbed hold of the younger fisher, and tossed him away as well. But it was as if the fishers had been thrown onto a trampoline. They both bounced right back to their feet and charged at the Great Bear, just as he was about to come at Morgan. Muskwa roared even louder as Mihko and Ochek grabbed hold of him again.

"Run, Morgan! Run!" Mihko shouted.

"We'll hold him off!" Ochek said.

Morgan heard the words, and she wanted to do exactly what Mihko had told her. She didn't think she could convince Muskwa to change. She didn't know who could. She didn't know who did. But her feet wouldn't budge; they were planted in place, like one of the roots from the trees surrounding her. She tried to command her legs to start moving, to run over to Eli, who was still standing off to the side. She wanted to take his hand and lead him away from the danger. But her legs wouldn't listen. All she could do was watch the fight unfold between the bear and the fishers, Mihko and Ochek attacking the beast with ferocity.

"Now!" Mihko said to her.

Morgan just shook her head in response. *I can't,* she thought, because even words wouldn't come. Her entire body was shaking with fear, as if she were standing outside in the middle of the White Time.

Ochek bit the great beast's arm, and Muskwa cried out in pain. The bite did nothing to stop him, though; it only made him angrier. Mihko went flying through the air, slamming against a tree and falling to its roots. Ochek bared his teeth and bit down again. Muskwa grunted, stumbled forward, ever closer to Morgan. He began to thrash madly at Ochek. Mihko wasn't getting back up.

"Morgan, get out of there!" Eli said.

She glanced at her brother, at Mihko, and then at Muskwa's arm, which was as thick as a young tree, raised up in the air. The last thing she saw was his furry brown arm hurtling towards her. The last thing she heard was Eli screaming. The last thing she felt was the impact to her head.

Then, she heard nothing, and everything was numb, and there was only darkness.

SEVENTEEN

Morgan could see only blackness, with her eyes closed or opened. Were her eyes closed? She was being held. She could feel her back against someone's lap, her neck against a soft and warm forearm, a hand set gently against the top of her head. She heard humming, distant at first, like a song being sung a mile away. The song became louder, and louder, until it was clear. It was the same song she'd heard from her mother. Was this what being dead felt like? Was it returning to the best memory, the only memory, of somebody you used to love? Somebody that, maybe, you still loved? Was it being in a darkened room, rocked by your mother, sung to, forever? Morgan waited to hear something else. The word that she'd heard each time she'd dreamed this same dream, remembered this same memory. *Kiskisitotaso. Do not forget yourself now that you are here with me. Nitanis. My daughter.*

"I won't forget myself," she whispered. "Not again."

But that word didn't come. No words came. Instead, a pain worse than she'd ever felt struck her head.

"What did she say?" came another voice. Not her mother's voice. It was a boy.

"Something about forgetting herself," said another voice. A woman's gentle voice, as soft and warm as the arm under the back of her neck.

"She's dreaming," the boy said. "Is she going to be okay?"

He sounded worried. Was he an angel? No. There would be no pain like this in heaven, in what the animal beings in Misewa called the Happy Hunting Grounds. And the pain was worsening, wrapping around her head and squeezing like a vise. Morgan cried out from the hurt. It pushed out the memories until only the darkness remained.

"Mihko, give her something for the pain."

"Ehe."

She heard these voices in the blackness, and then rustling. People were moving around. She felt smooth wood against her mouth, and then a cool, bitter liquid slipping between her lips, pooling against her tongue.

"Drink this," he said.

It hurt to do everything. It hurt to think. It hurt to move. It hurt to swallow. Morgan tried to take the liquid down her throat. But she coughed, which sent another spark of pain through her head. The wood touched her lips again, and then she felt a paw over her mouth, a breath against her face. It made her swallow, no matter how much it hurt.

"I'm sorry, Morgan."

She choked. She tried to cough it out. But the medicine forced its way down her throat. She felt it, the cold sensation, move all the way into her chest. Soon after, the rustling stopped. Whoever was with her had quit moving around. They were talking, but their voices moved farther away.

"Don't go," she whispered. "Don't let me go."

Then they left, despite her pleading. They were gone, and so was the pain. So was the song. All that was left was the darkness.

When she came to again, the first thing Morgan felt was how dry her mouth was, but, she thought, she'd take that sensation over the intense pain she'd felt during her brief moments of consciousness earlier. That was a pain she'd not wish on her worst enemy. Now more lucid, she realized that she'd woken up before. She was not dead. She had not found herself in heaven, in the arms of her mother. Of course not. Her mother was alive. How could she have been in the Happy Hunting Grounds? She'd not been right in the head. Who would have been, with that sort of pain? But then, who'd been holding her? Who'd been singing? Was that part of the dream? Was that real?

"Unnnh," Morgan groaned.

Slowly, hesitantly, she blinked her eyes open. It was dark except for the flickering light of a nearby fire. Sitting around it were Mihko, Ochek, and Eli. Morgan was relieved to see that Mihko and Ochek were okay after the beating they'd taken.

Eli was the first to notice that Morgan had stirred. He rushed to her, knelt beside her.

"Morgan, you're okay," he said.

She pushed herself up onto her elbows and shimmied back until her head could rest on the root of a tree. Propped up, she could fully see their makeshift campsite. A few feet from the fire, on the other side of it from Morgan, was a tent the group had constructed. A spit had been made and on it hung some meat. They'd been having supper. The pain was gone, but her appetite had not come in its place. She didn't feel at all like eating. She did, however, feel like water. Her mouth felt like stone, and, worse yet, the bitter after-taste of the medicine lingered against her tongue.

"Water," she said. "Can I have some water?"

"Yes, of course."

Eli squeezed her hand, as though to assure her he would return, before leaving to fetch her a leather flask. He was back seconds later, and he dipped the flask towards her mouth, letting the water spill past her lips, and, though she didn't much care, over her face.

When she'd had enough, she nodded, and Eli took the flask away.

"Thank you."

"Don't thank me," he said despondently. "I just stood there while you got hurt . . . and he could've . . . you wouldn't have . . ." His voice began to sound frantic.

She put her hand against his cheek and managed to smile. "Breathe, Eli. Take a deep breath in through your nose, and let it out through your mouth. Calm down." It was something she'd done countless times before, and she knew it worked.

He did what she said, and soon his nerves seemed to relax.

"You couldn't have done anything to stop him," she said,

"or you would've been hurt too, or worse. I was stupid; I shouldn't have gone. I just thought . . ."

"That you could get through to him."

"I should've listened to you. That's all. Please don't beat yourself up."

Eli leaned over and gave her a very careful hug, as though the blow to her head had turned her to glass. "I thought he'd killed you. I really thought he had."

"I know," she said, "but I'm okay. Okay?"

Eli straightened. He wiped at his cheeks. "Okay."

"What happened anyway?"

Eli told Morgan how, after she'd been knocked out by the blow from Muskwa's arm, which had been meant for Ochek, her head had jerked to the side and she'd collapsed, lifeless. He'd thought then that she was dead. She'd lain there on her side, unconscious, and the Great Bear had flung Ochek away a final time. Then he'd walked up to Morgan, rolled her onto her back so that her face was pointed towards the sky, and leaned towards her. He'd put his nose right up to her, and just looked at her. He'd looked at her for what seemed like hours, but in reality had likely been only seconds. "Leave her alone!" Eli had demanded. Muskwa had taken one last look at her, grunted, then stepped over her and continued on his way. He hadn't finished her off. He hadn't bothered himself further with the fishers. He hadn't even acknowledged Eli.

"Why?" Morgan asked.

"Maybe we didn't have anything he wanted," Eli mused.

When he'd been sure that the bear wasn't going to circle around and return, he'd rushed over to his sister, and was soon joined by the two animal beings, roughed up, but that was all. He'd checked for a pulse, and found that her heart was still beating. *Thump, thump, thump, thump, thump, thump, thump.* He'd put his ear right close to her mouth, just to be sure, and felt her breath against his skin.

"We carried you back here," Eli continued, "and then—"

"I heard a voice," Morgan said. "I heard a woman humming a song that I know. Was I dreaming? Was I . . . ?" She covered her face with her hand and closed her eyes, trying to go back to that moment.

"Ochek ran back to Misewa because Mihko needed some medicines," Eli explained, "and Nicky came. She wouldn't leave until she knew you were settled. Until you could really rest."

That explained why the memory, this time, felt more real than ever before. Nicky had cradled her in her arms. Nicky had sung her a song. Maybe the dream part of it was the song Morgan had heard—maybe she'd heard what she'd wanted to hear. And maybe she could hear what she wanted to again. After all, she did have her mother's name and number. She just needed to not hang up on her next time.

"How are you feeling?"

Morgan shrugged. "Alive."

"We could go back to the village, you know. Mihko said we could, if we wanted."

"No," she said. "I don't want to go back. Besides, it's not like we're going to chase down a bear again. We're going to check a bunch of traps."

Eli didn't say anything. Morgan looked at him suspiciously.

"*Right?* We're going to check traps?" She got to her feet.

She felt dizzy. He supported her until she steadied herself. She put her hands on her hips. "Right, Eli?"

"I . . ."

"Oh god, that's so annoying!" Morgan pushed past Eli and walked right up to the fire, standing over the fishers. "*Excuse* me."

"Morgan, you look good as new," Ochek said.

"What's going on?" she asked. "Where are we going?"

"To the trapline?" Ochek said innocently.

"Bull! Somebody just answer me already!"

"Muskwa wasn't headed towards Misewa," Mihko said.

"Yeah, that's good, isn't it?"

"He will, though," Ochek said. "He always does when he comes to the southern woods."

"He will," Mihko agreed, "but for now, he looked to be headed towards our friends' village, Otakosík, southwest of here."

"They want to help, if they can," Eli said, then added quietly, "if *we* can."

"What?" Morgan said. "Help how? He just kicked our butts! How are you going to help? You just said you don't even try to stop him when he comes to Misewa! And Eli, you just stood there. How are *you* going to help? I did too! How am *I* going to help!"

"Breathe in through—"

"*Don't,* Eli."

"I don't know how we're going to help," Mihko said. "Maybe it's too late. But maybe, just maybe, we can get there before him."

"He *was* taking his time," Ochek added.

"They don't have somebody like Pip to alert them. It's a small village. But if we know he's headed there, we can't turn our backs to them."

Morgan walked away from the fire and stood at the end of the clearing. She stared out into the forest.

Eli came to join her. "What do you want to do?" he asked.

Everything she remembered about her encounter with Muskwa replayed in her mind. And everything Eli had said to her before she ran off, stupidly, to try to reason with the bear.

"Before," she said, "you were saying something about how Mason could be dead in *our* present but still not have come to Misewa in this past? Or something like that?"

"Yeah. We've already done everything that we've done in Misewa," Eli said. "We found Askí in the White Time, we saved Misewa, we saw Ochek die. That's *our* past, but it's *their* future. It'll happen for them someday, but it's happened for us already."

"So, the short, uncomplicated answer is that we can die here and nothing will change the fact that their future is inevitable."

"We can die here."

Morgan stared into the darkness, into the deep black that only the woods could offer. Before, the dark had terrified her. Now, she knew she could walk right into it and not be afraid.

And then everything they'd been through in the White Time forced its way into her brain. They—Eli and Morgan—hadn't thought they could help, but then they had. And what if they hadn't? Where would Misewa be? By now, their relatives would be dead, and the North Country would still be stuck in the White Time.

Mihko was right. If they could help, they had to help. The fishers, Eli, and her.

"Maybe they need us," she said. "Maybe *this* is why we're here."

"Maybe."

She sighed, resigned to what she felt they needed to do. "We're literally going to go after a big, mean bear."

She and Eli walked back to the fire together, where the fishers had been waiting anxiously for the siblings' answer, for time was getting short.

"You can wait for us back in Misewa," Ochek said. "It's alright."

"We haven't come a long way just to turn back now," Eli said. "And not just from Misewa."

"The Great Bear didn't kill me when he could have, right?" Morgan said. "He didn't kill any of us."

"No. No, he didn't," Mihko said. "Maybe you were right. Maybe there's good in him."

"Well," Morgan said, "let's go find out."

When had danger ever stopped them before?

EIGHTEEN

Minutes later, the camp was packed up, and the group left for Otakosík, hoping to get there before Muskwa. It was deep in the night, and the sun wouldn't be up for several hours. Before dousing the fire, they made torches out of cloth wrapped tightly around wood. The cloth had been dipped in grease so that it would burn longer. Otakosík was beyond Mihko's trapline, and while Morgan and Eli, and undoubtedly Ochek and Mihko, could have found their way to the trapline with their eyes closed, it would be good to have the extra light.

It wasn't long before they came to the tree bridge over the canyon. It looked exactly the same as it would years in the future, Morgan thought, but this time, thankfully, there was no wind or snow or ice to make the task of crossing harder. Morgan was far more confident about crossing thawed-out tree bridges.

They walked to the edge. Far below, the river ran east. Eli looked down despondently, and Morgan knew why.

Mahihkan had fallen into those very waters, having saved them from Mason's arrows.

"You okay?" she asked.

"Yeah," he said. "It's just that . . ."

"I know. It's hard to think of him down there."

Eli just nodded.

Morgan pictured not a wolf, but rather Mason's body passing by, carried that way by the swift water. But she didn't offer him more than a passing thought. He didn't deserve more than that. Instead, she imagined the river down below frozen, covered in snow, and her own body lying there, lifeless. Her eyes trailed up, and that imagined body floated through the air, up towards the tree bridge. She was hanging there, her legs flailing wildly, her fingers clutching a crack in the wood.

"I should've died, you know," Morgan said. "I mean, on our first trip here, not yesterday. Yesterday too, but . . ."

"But you didn't," Eli said. "Either time."

It was only by luck that she was here today.

"Come on, you two," said Mihko, who, with his son, had been waiting at the foot of the bridge to cross. "We've no time to spare."

"You're not afraid of heights, are you?" Ochek asked, and he ran across the bridge as though it were a sidewalk on a city street.

"No," Morgan said, quietly enough that only Eli could hear. "I'm not."

She left the edge of the canyon and followed Mihko across it. Eli crossed last.

Once on the other side, Morgan knew that they'd arrived on Mihko's trapline even before Mihko announced it.

They walked past the spot where Ochek would one day construct a camp within the trees to protect it from the elements. They walked into the bush, lush and alive and painted warm colors by torchlight, humbled by the towering trees overhead. Still, those trees were nothing against the giant sequoia Ochek had climbed to release the summer birds, or the Great Tree itself.

She and Eli followed Mihko and Ochek deeper into the forest on the other side of the canyon, heading west, closer to the heart of the trapline and, beyond it, Otakosík.

Their pace, steady and determined, didn't let up as they made their way across the trapline. There were no detours to check for game if the snare or trap was too far out of the way; doing so felt like leaving the village at risk. But some traps were accessible, and Mihko and Ochek went to gather the game where possible, telling the siblings to keep going and they would catch up. They always did; the fishers never spent more than a moment, experts as they were, collecting the game and resetting a trap or snare. And it was important to gather this food—for Misewa, yes, but for the other village as well. Because if Muskwa had already been there, if the Great Bear had already done his terrible work, the villagers would need sustenance until they could catch their own game again.

Soon they were through the trapline, and eventually they came to a clearing where the horizon was clear in the distance. Over the line of trees and below the sky, there rose an autumn glow. Morgan thought it was beautiful, and, even in this desperate time, allowed herself to admire it. How often did she see things like this on her world, after all? The warmth swelling out like blood from the heart of the land.

"The sunrise is so pretty," she remarked, thinking, at the same time, that they'd walked through the night and now morning was upon them.

"But that's not right," Eli said.

"No, it's not right at all," Ochek said.

"What are you talking about?" Morgan asked. "That's clearly the sunrise."

"The sun rises in the east, Morgan," Mihko said.

"Oh my god," she said. "It totally does."

They all stopped right there, in the clearing between the forest and the canyon, just past Mihko's trapline. They all looked off in the distance, at the colors hovering over the tree line like a cloud, seeing how that cloud seemed to be floating from one place. One area on the ground. Morgan looked carefully, and noticed something like a tail trailing from the colors all the way to Askí.

"What is it, then?" she asked.

At that moment, as though in response to Morgan's question, they heard what sounded like the shrill call of a distant cricket. Far off and unthreatening. But it was enough for Mihko to scan the area for the source of it. Morgan, Eli, and Ochek did the same, but nobody saw anything until the sound came again, this time closer and more piercing. In the direction of the sound, a tiny orange light was visible that grew and grew until it became clear that it was a fire. Somebody was running towards them with a torch.

"Help! Somebody help!" a female voice was calling out, and whoever it was, she sounded terrified.

"Over here!" Ochek said.

"Oh, thank Creator! Thank the Creator above! He's come! He's come again!"

Morgan knew the voice, and soon enough everybody saw who it was. Emerging from the darkness with a torch in hand, her clothes ripped and burned, her eyes filled with terror, panting and wild, was Arikwachas. The colors hadn't been the sunrise, and they hadn't been the swelling heart of the land either. It was Otakosík burning, its flames rising into the sky.

"We're too late," Mihko said.

NINETEEN

Resisting the impulse to hug Arik was made easier by how panicked she was, how disheveled she looked, the gravity of the situation. Morgan couldn't think of a single time she had ever seen Arik act anything like this. Not when Mason was shooting arrows at them. Not when they were in the boat crossing the lake after stealing the summer birds. Not when they were trapped at the canyon, having found out that the ice bridge had melted away. The animal being, as soon as she skidded to a stop at the group, tossed her torch to the ground and buckled over, bracing herself with her paws on her knees.

"Is everybody safe?" Ochek asked.

"How bad is it in the village?" Mihko asked.

"Well, presently, at this moment right now"—she looked back in the direction she'd just come—"there isn't quite an Otakosík anymore. Not really." Arik pulled at her ripped and singed clothing. "I just barely escaped with my life. Longhouses are getting ransacked, food stores are getting eaten, villagers are running for the woods to save their lives . . ."

The elder fisher, looking as determined as one can look, started off in the direction that Arik had just run from. Morgan, Arik, Eli, and Ochek stood there for a few seconds, staring at each other. None of them moved, until Mihko stopped several yards away.

"Let's go! We can still do something to help!"

"Why would we go to Otakosík when Muskwa has already done what he set out to do?" Ochek asked. "Shouldn't we go back to Misewa?"

"Did you not hear what I just said?" Even in the dark of night, Morgan could tell that Mihko's steely eyes were aimed directly at Ochek. He softened his tone. "My son. Misewa is our home. Misewa is our family. But all the beings in the North Country are our community, are our relatives. If the Great Bear has not left—or if he has, and there is still something we can do—then we must."

"Ehe, Nipapa," Ochek said.

"Astum."

Mihko continued walking towards Otakosík. Ochek followed his father, and Arik seemed happy to follow Ochek and Mihko, even though she'd just run from that very direction. She skipped away from the two humans and caught up to Ochek. The siblings quickened their pace to catch up with the animal beings, who were far enough ahead of them at this point that they'd almost disappeared into the night. Morgan was exhausted, and some of the pain was returning, in particular a rather unpleasant headache, but she didn't let that stop her. Helping a village that had just been ransacked, however they were able, seemed more important than needing a Tylenol and a good nap.

Less than half an hour later, the five travelers came upon Otakosík. From a distance, on the horizon, it had looked like a rising sun. As they drew closer, it became apparent that the beauty was born of destruction. Otakosík was burning to the ground. From what Morgan could see, the village was smaller than Misewa. She wondered how many animal beings lived there, but that number was currently impossible to know, because there wasn't a soul around. Thankfully, it appeared the Great Bear had left as well. Of course he was gone, Morgan thought. There was nothing left for Muskwa to destroy. No food left for him to eat. Nothing here, now, that he needed.

There appeared to have been four longhouses, three of them quite close together. Morgan figured that these three dwellings were for the regular community members. They had all been torn apart and set on fire. One had so far stubbornly refused to fall but looked as though it might at any moment. Almost an entire side of it had been torn apart and they could see right inside, where the furniture, shelving, and clothing had all been ruined. A wooden bench had fallen into the firepit. A meat rack at the front door was empty and shattered. It looked like an abandoned game of pick-a-stick. The other two longhouses were nothing but piles of charcoal strewn across the ground, low flames glowing to reveal the suggestion of what they had once been. Farther on, no more than thirty yards away, was the fourth longhouse. It was in no better condition than the others, half standing and half fallen. The fallen sections revealed the inside walls, which displayed drawings in ocher. A history lost. Against her better judgment, Morgan approached the longhouse until she was close enough to see the drawings more clearly, before they succumbed to the flames. It was like hearing somebody's dying breath.

"Come, Morgan," Mihko said. "There's nothing here. Nobody to help."

"There's not nothing," Morgan said. "It's got the drawings on the walls, just like the Council Hut in Misewa."

"Yes, it does."

"Well . . ." Morgan caught herself. Her breath had started to quicken. A knot had formed somewhere deep in her chest. "This longhouse is going to burn down and all the paintings on the walls are, like, their history, and when they all burn up, that history's going to be gone, and . . ." Morgan took a deep, calming breath. "It just sucks, I guess."

"It does . . . suck . . . that these structures will fall, and with them, the paintings that have documented Otakosík's history." There was a broken piece of wall on the ground near the longhouse. Mihko picked it up and looked at the partial drawing. "These"—Mihko tossed it back to the ground—"these are just drawings. They're important, but their history doesn't die with them. In all of our communities across the North Country, knowledge keepers are entrusted with passing down our history from one generation to the next. In our village, the knowledge keeper is Chief Wapistan. If the walls of the Council Hut were ever to fall, it would be the stories he holds that would allow us to draw that history again. One day, when he makes his journey to the Happy Hunting Grounds, another will keep that history alive by remembering the stories and telling them to others."

"Really?" she asked. "They won't lose any of this?"

"A house is a house, Morgan. It's not a home." He pointed to his heart. "A home is in here, along with all the stories. That's why they're kept where they are, because they cannot be broken down, burned, or taken away." Mihko gently pulled Morgan away from the longhouse. "Now, before all those paintings fall to the ground and crush you underneath their weight, why don't you come back with the rest of us."

At that moment, part of the ceiling collapsed, and some debris narrowly missed Morgan's legs.

"Yeah," she said, "that's probably a good idea."

The five beings congregated back near the three longhouses, their impromptu meeting well lit by the burning remains of the village. It was hot, as though it were not a very late hour on an autumn night, but rather a clear day in the summer. Their bodies cast long shadows away from the village.

"What now?" Ochek asked after a prolonged silence.

"I can't say I'm all that upset about missing the Great Bear after he nearly killed me." Arik looked over the ruins. "I suppose I'll have to help rebuild this place if I expect them to let me stay again."

Mihko's voice was like a growl, low and angry. "They'll have to rebuild it again and again, just as we will have to rebuild Misewa when Muskwa comes."

"I prefer to look on the bright side," Arik said. "It's a chance to make improvements!"

Mihko looked once more at the devastation the Great Bear had caused, then turned away. "He will never stop."

"Sooo . . . ," Arik said.

"We need to head back to Misewa before Muskwa gets there."

"Or we could just, you know, wait until he's been there and help rebuild it too," Arik offered. "Just think of all the renovations we could make. Those birds live in such primitive houses up there in the trees, don't they? And I've noticed a few loose floorboards and—"

"Misewa won't need rebuilding," Mihko said defiantly. "Not one more time."

"What?" Ochek said. "Are we going to move it or something before he gets there?"

"This girl"—Mihko pointed at Morgan—"this girl, who has lived with us for five weeks, ran off to stop the Great Bear."

"She did?" Arik asked. "Way to go, Iskwésis!" She looked Morgan over, very likely taking in the fact that Morgan was tired and pained, and noting that Otakosík had just been demolished. "I mean, you obviously didn't succeed, but you're also not dead. On balance, that's impressive."

"That's not the point!" Mihko said. "All we've ever done is run from him. We've never tried to stand up, all of us, together, and fight. Not until now."

"But you said a home was in *here*," Morgan said, pointing to her heart.

"That I did," Mihko admitted. "But if we can save our village, if we can protect the people within it, well . . . there'll be another story for the next generation, won't there?"

They left immediately for Misewa—not to run from the Great Bear, but to stand against him. Morgan and Eli followed the animal beings dutifully; of course, there was no way they weren't going to do whatever they could to help. Morgan was convinced more than ever that this was a moment in time that was necessary, to lead Askí to the future they'd already experienced. That even if her future, and Eli's, were uncertain, they had always decided to help, and their help would lead to a positive outcome for Misewa against the Great Bear. An outcome that would one day ensure the villagers' health and safety. Their ability to live the good life.

If she had to die for something, she was ready to die for that.

TWENTY

Mihko was racing ahead as though he were possessed, and keeping up a breakneck pace through the southern woods towards Misewa. He was like the fisher version of the Terminator. As day broke, Morgan wondered if they were going to stop at all, or walk straight through without rest or food in order to get to the village before Muskwa did. She couldn't help but feel disappointed in Muskwa for causing all of this fear and chaos, even though she knew that he would change in the coming years. Beside her, to her left, walking quickly but still managing to make it seem leisurely, was Arik. To her right was Eli, and ahead of them was Ochek.

"Tansi, little humans," Arik said. "With all this walking, there's time to properly introduce ourselves."

"Little humans! You're Eli's size!" Morgan laughed.

"Okay, that's fair," Arik said. "But I meant 'children' when I called you 'little humans,' in my defense."

"It's good to meet you," Eli said.

"Yeah," Morgan said. "I just wish it were under different circumstances."

"I do too, children. But you know what they say, don't you? When you find Labrador leaves, you make Labrador tea."

"Nobody says that," Ochek said without looking back.

"Oh, stop being so grumpy, young fisher," Arik said.

"Well, they don't," Ochek said defensively.

"I do," Arik said.

"On earth we say something about lemons," Eli said. "When life hands you lemons, make lemonade."

"Is lemonade good?"

Eli nodded. "It's sweet."

"Well, so is Labrador tea," Arik said proudly.

"It's not sweet," Ochek said.

"*Okay,*" Arik groaned. "Honestly. I meant that the tea is good is all."

"We know what you meant," Morgan said.

"I like you children already, I think," Arik said. "And this earth place."

"We like you too," Eli said. "Meeting you has made the last day less awful."

"Well, aren't you sweet like lemonade," Arik said. "You're Eli, correct?"

"Yeah," Eli said.

"And you are . . ."

"Morgan."

"I'm pleased to meet you, not-so-little humans," Arik said. "I'm Arikwachas, but these two animal beings here"—she gave Mihko, still far ahead of the others, and Ochek what appeared to be a mock glare—"know that I don't like being called that. You can call me—"

"Arik!" Morgan blurted out.

"Yes . . . that's right. How would you know that?"

"Oh, I . . ." Morgan found herself scrambling again. "I've noticed that the animal beings here tend to, like, shorten their names sometimes. Like if people called me Morg." *Morg. Morgue.* She smiled at the memory of telling Emily to call her that.

"Morg." Arik nodded thoughtfully. "Makes sense. Do you want me to call you that?"

"No, no, no," Morgan said quickly. "You can call me Morgan. Fully Morgan."

"Morgan it is," Arik said.

"There's no way you can shorten Eli," Eli said.

"Well, there's E, if you wanted to get really efficient," Arik mused.

"E equals mc squared." Morgan snickered. "I should start calling you that."

"No, you should absolutely not ever call me that."

"Plus that *lengthens* his name, doesn't it?" Arik pointed out. "That's not the same thing."

"*And* it's stupid," Eli said. "Maybe it would make sense if I were good at math, but that's your thing, *Morg*."

"Somebody's salty," Morgan said.

"I know it's only been a short while, but I think we're going to get along just fine," Arik said.

"I think that's a good bet," Morgan said.

"Do you see, young fisher?" Arik called up to Ochek, who was several feet ahead of them. "They've been through exactly what you've been through and they're just as pleasant as can be. I find that, in hard times, being nice can make things a little less hard."

"I'm just annoyed at my dad, okay?" Ochek said. "Running ahead and yelling at me in front of everybody. It's embarrassing. He's just so . . . intense sometimes."

Morgan snorted, trying to hold in laughter.

"What?" Ochek snapped.

"Nothing." Morgan pictured young Ochek as the grizzled, older version of himself. "Don't worry about it."

"You can't just say 'nothing' after you obviously meant something."

Ochek crossed his arms while he walked. Past Ochek and present Ochek both pouted—that was something they had in common at least. But Morgan wasn't sure if she'd ever get used to teenager Ochek. It was just too weird. He would have fit right in at school, sitting in the lunchroom, eating with the jocks. She laughed again at that thought. A humanoid fisher eating french fries and a Pizza Pop from the cafeteria.

"It's just," Morgan said, "I get embarrassed by my foster parents. I can relate. It's funny when you see, like, an anthropomorphic animal doing it."

"Anthropo-what?"

"It's like when something, like an animal, has human characteristics." When Morgan saw Ochek's confused face, she rephrased it. "When an animal, like you or Arik, for example, can walk and talk and do stuff that four-legged ones can't." She thought that throwing in Askí terminology—"four-legged ones"—would help. It seemed to. Ochek nodded.

"How old's your dad?" Eli asked.

"Old. I don't know. Not as old as Arik."

"Oh, he's just a kit compared to me," Arik agreed.

"And how old are you, Arik?" Morgan asked.

"As old as the trees, children. As old as the sky is blue . . ." Arik scratched her head. "Wait, that doesn't make sense. Let's stick with trees. But then again, it's not how old you are, it's how old you feel, little ones."

"I wish you guys had driver's licenses or something," Morgan said. "I mean, how do you know when it's your birthday?"

"There you go with your earth words again," Arik said. "I can guess what a birthday is: the day one is born. But what's a driver's license?"

Morgan took a minute to explain how people drove vehicles on earth—they didn't walk everywhere—and how you needed to have a driver's license if you wanted to operate a car. She even went into unnecessary details, like how you get a learner's permit first, and then you have to take a road test to get an actual license. Arik nodded during the whole explanation.

The sun rose and morning came and there was no rest in sight for any of them, as Mihko pressed on to Misewa. The children found it difficult to keep up with him, and even the other two animal beings appeared to have trouble. At times he got so far ahead that he threatened to disappear into the trees. He seemed to just trust that they'd all keep pace with him. What a surprise he was in for, Morgan thought, because she wasn't sure that she could walk much longer. She was soaked with sweat, her legs were sore, her knees were shaking from exhaustion, and she felt as though she could barely catch her breath. Plus, she was fairly certain that she'd sustained at least a minor concussion from Muskwa. The daylight was bothering her, and throughout this walk she'd lost her balance more than once. She was about to call out to Mihko and beg him to slow down, allow them to rest for at least a little while, when he came to an abrupt stop ahead.

When the four stragglers caught up to him, he held a hand up to warn them to be quiet.

Muskwa was sitting on the ground in a small clearing, stoking a fire. This was the Muskwa that Morgan knew. He looked calm and harmless, taking great care to tend the fire. And he looked thoughtful, watching the flames as though they had a story to tell. She had it in her mind that she would try again, that she would walk into the open area and reason with the Great Bear. Maybe she'd just attempted to stop him at the wrong time. She would find in him the Chief he would become one day. She started forward but instantly felt Mihko's paw pressed against her stomach to hold her back.

"No, Morgan," Mihko whispered. "Not this time."

Morgan looked at Muskwa, just thirty feet away, sitting peacefully on the ground in the deep and cool grass that glistened in the light of the early fall morning. Staring thoughtfully at the dwindling flames, nudging the burning wood with a twig. She couldn't believe it. She couldn't believe that this animal being was responsible for so much destruction. But she'd seen it with her own eyes.

She stayed where she was.

"Okay," she whispered, "you win. But we still need to get around him, don't we?"

"That we do."

Mihko placed his back against the trunk of the large tree they'd been huddled around to stay out of sight of the Great Bear. He slid to the ground and sat there. And, just as before, the others followed his lead and sat down to create a circle of weary travelers. There, they were not only out of sight but downwind, assured that their scent wouldn't carry to the bear's keen nose. And so they seemed to be safe, until they were ready to move.

"And the plan might be . . . ?" Arik whispered after a long silence.

Mihko's response was brief and direct. "When he goes to sleep, we'll walk around him and keep going. Bears like to sleep during the day and look for food in the night."

"He certainly had his fill last night," Arik whispered.

So they waited. They waited and waited and waited. And there wasn't much to do while they waited, because they couldn't make a sound for fear they might alert Muskwa to their presence. According to Mihko, bears had excellent hearing, along with their strong sense of smell. And so the five of them hunkered down and watched Muskwa to see when he'd decide to have a nap.

Eventually the fire died, and not long after the last flame flickered out, Muskwa lay down. Still, the waiting continued until snoring rumbled through the silence. Then, and only then, did they move from their spot by the tree. They stood up together, and, still together, they inched forward. Muskwa's belly rose and fell like a giant wave. Even his snoring shook the ground. Arik volunteered to venture into the clearing and check just how deeply asleep Muskwa was before they continued on their way to Misewa.

Arik tiptoed across the long grass towards the Great Bear, and once there, the squirrel skittered around him in a huge circle. She leaned over to where his head was, and waved a paw just inches from his face. All of this felt like enough to prove he was sleeping soundly, that they could pass him easily and get a head start to Misewa. But for some reason, probably because she never knew when enough was enough, Arik picked up the stick Muskwa had used to stoke the fire and poked him with it.

"Oh my god, she is *literally* poking the bear!" Morgan shout-whispered. "You never poke the bear!"

Muskwa snorted. He groaned. He rolled over onto his side. He swatted at the area where Arik had poked him with the stick.

During all of this, nobody breathed. Morgan imagined Muskwa reaching out, grabbing Arik, and putting her into his mouth all at once. But he didn't. Everybody and everything froze, including Muskwa, and then the Great Bear started to snore again. Arik shrugged, then scurried back to the group.

"That was stupid," Ochek said.

"I agree with my son," Mihko said. "All you had to do was check and see if Muskwa was actually asleep or not."

"Gotta go with the fishers here," Morgan said.

"Me too," Eli said.

"Well, you're all no fun," Arik said. "Besides, now we know, for certain, that we can just walk by and be on our way, can't we?"

At the very least, the other four had to agree. The Great Bear was fast asleep, full from the enormous meal he'd consumed at Otakosík before destroying it. The group walked quickly but quietly around the perimeter of the clearing. Even with Muskwa sleeping, it was nerve-racking. Somebody stepped on a twig, which made them all stop and hold their breath. Near the edge of the clearing, when they'd almost made it through, Morgan tripped and fell into Eli; more balance issues. In turn, Eli almost fell into Arik, and it nearly became a disastrous game of dominoes. But eventually, they made it through.

Once they were a safe distance away, they double-timed it to Misewa. Even Morgan managed to keep pace with Mihko now. Time was on their side, but there wasn't much of it.

TWENTY-ONE

The sun had climbed to its noon height by the time the five weary travelers returned to Misewa, having walked through the southern woods all morning without stopping to sleep or eat. Morgan was sure that even Mihko would have rested if he'd felt there was a choice, but with Muskwa sleeping, Misewa had the valuable advantage of time to prepare for what lay ahead. Because the Great Bear was indeed coming. According to Mihko, this happened every few seasons. And if more proof was needed, Muskwa had taken a nap in a clearing that lay between Otakosík and Misewa; it was obvious what direction he was headed.

"Are you nervous about Muskwa?" Morgan asked Eli, privately, as they entered the village.

"Yes," Eli said. "I'm not sure how you couldn't be."

"They're going to have to fight him if they're going to save Misewa. That *huge* bear. And that means we're going to have to help them fight."

"I know. And I'm going to have to do something more than just stand there and look stupid."

"You didn't just . . ." She stopped herself, because he *had* just stood there. He may not have looked stupid, just frightened, but the fact remained.

"Maybe that's all I'm capable of doing," he said. "It's exactly what I did after school when those bullies took my drawing pad."

"Eli, you're capable of lots, and you know it. Everybody gets scared."

"Are you scared? You were going to try and talk to Muskwa again last night. How scared can you be?"

"Of course I'm scared. I don't want to die. And I don't want to make the wrong decision and change the future somehow. I'm, like, extra scared."

"If things work the way they're supposed to work, then we always make the same decision anyway."

"So how do we know what that decision is so we don't mess up?" she asked. "See, we should've talked about time travel! Who cares if it's boring."

"Honestly, I'm more worried about whether we live or die than what we're supposed to do." Eli smiled unconvincingly in a bad attempt at softening what he'd said. "I think all we need to do is what feels right. Just . . . listen to our hearts or something."

"Wow." Morgan patted Eli's shoulder. "Somehow you managed to say something super cheesy after saying something super morbid. I don't think that's ever been done before in the history of conversations."

"Thanks," he said. "I've never set a world record before."

"I guess, even if their future is certain," she said, "it's not certain *how* it's certain. I think the only thing that's *certain* certain is that we're a part of what they do, and we'll just do it, because we're in the past and it's already been done. It works out, live or die."

Eli nudged Morgan's hip and smiled, this time convincingly. "I just want to point out that somehow I managed to understand what you were saying, and also that you managed to say 'certain' a million times in one sentence, and I don't think that's ever been done before in the history of conversations."

"Look at us, both setting world records." But she smiled too as they walked up to the fishers' longhouse. "Maybe it's best that we don't know what to do, or how it happens."

"Maybe so," he said.

Although they'd decided that they would take part in the fight against Muskwa, in whatever way they were asked, they were not invited to the Council meeting to discuss strategy. Although they were community members in Misewa in the present, here in the past they were relative strangers, even after the weeks they'd been in the village. So they watched what took place from outside the fishers' longhouse.

The community-wide meeting was set up in the circular clearing in front of the Council Hut, surrounded by the seven longhouses and the teepees. Above, up high, the seven Bird Warriors stood outside of their dwellings and watched, silently but with great interest.

It was a meeting like Morgan had never seen before in Misewa. From what she knew, meetings that involved Chief and Council took place inside the Council Hut, were quiet and calm, and had an order about them. This meeting was nothing like that. Though it opened, as usual, with a prayer, it quickly turned into a heated discussion. The villagers argued about whether they would run away and allow Muskwa to do what he had just done to Otakosík or stay and fight. Fight. Something they hadn't done before. At least not against the Great Bear. Would the village try and stop Muskwa from ruining their longhouses, tearing down the teepees, eating all their food stores? Would the village try and stop the Great Bear from forcing Misewa to start all over again, to rebuild the village from the ashes he would leave behind?

It seemed, to Morgan, as she and Eli observed from outside the circle, that the majority of the villagers wanted to leave and allow Muskwa to tear Misewa to pieces. They were used to it. He'd come countless times before, and they'd rebuilt Misewa each time. At least, the argument went, if they ran away and waited to come back when the Great Bear had left, there would be no loss of life.

"If we stay and fight and he kills us all, there'll be nobody to rebuild our homes anyway!" shouted Ahtik, the caribou.

"Ehe! Better to live and rebuild than die and have no work left to do!" called out Amisk, the beaver, with a slap of their tail for good measure.

"We should've left right after Nicky warned us! Muskwa could be here any moment!" another cried.

"The nomads have already abandoned their teepees!" argued yet another.

"We've wasted time!"

"Enough!" Mihko emerged from the crowd to stand before Chief and Council. "Enough of this cowardice." He turned from the community's leadership and paced back and forth in front of the crowd. "Our answer has always been to run. Always. As though all we have are hind legs to flee, but no arms with which to fight! I say enough. Muskwa comes, and we run and hide. We let him have what he wants, destroying everything we've worked to build in the process. We used to be warriors! Because of the actions of one being—no matter how terrible, no matter how big, no matter how frightening he may be—we've changed who we are. We can't continue to let another dictate who we are because we choose fear. Fear of him, yes, but fear of who we are, who we used to be." Mihko turned once more to face Chief and Council. "I say no more. I say we stand up against Muskwa, once and for all."

Morgan was captivated by Mihko's words. She took her eyes off the elder fisher only to see how the other villagers, and Chief and Council, were reacting. But when he spoke of Muskwa changing who the villagers were, who they *are*, she found herself looking right at Eli and thinking about how he had cut his hair. She knew that long, braided hair meant something more than just style for Indigenous people. It meant something culturally and spiritually, and made people just like Eli, like her, feel strong and proud. Was what Eli had done any different from what most of the villagers wanted to do upon hearing that Muskwa was on his way?

But what a speech, she thought, because Morgan had seen some villagers in the crowd nodding, villagers who had previously supported the idea of running and hiding. And Eli, who had spent most of his time in the North Country with his hood up, pulled it off.

The village meeting fell silent as Chief and Council quietly conferred. They had heard all the arguments, both for and against the idea of leaving Misewa. They had been presented with the two options—stay and fight, or run and hide—and the decision now fell to them. Morgan knew that whatever they decided, the villagers would be bound by it. That was the way it had always been, as far back as time went, and the way it would always be, deep into the future. Wapistan and his trusted companions talked for a long time, long enough that when they finished their deliberations, the sun had started to fall, dipping towards the horizon. To Morgan, it meant that Muskwa couldn't be that far.

"Pisiskowak! Animals of Misewa!" Wapistan's voice boomed, surprising from one who seemed so old and delicate. "These are times of trouble, there is little doubt. And they are times we've known before. Yes, the nomads have left, but they have that luxury. The land and the land alone is their home. Not this place." Wapistan scanned the crowd, from left to right. "We do not have that same luxury. This place is our home, and so it will always be. Yes, Muskwa comes, and with him, fear. You want to run. Even the bravest of us may feel that fear. Your body shakes. But we cannot let fear tell us what to do any longer. Mihko is right. We have run for too long, even though we are in the same place. It's time for us to lay claim to this place for good. It's time for us to break through these times of trouble, no matter the cost. The strongest will stand to protect our village.

The rest of us will be brought to safety until we can return, with the hope that we will not have to leave again. That this place will always be a place of safety."

"We have to move quickly." Oho took over from Wapistan, as the Chief now looked exhausted, as though it had taken everything he had in him to speak those words. "Now is not the time to hesitate, for we know *who* comes but we do not know when. *Who*, then, will stand against this menace, and *who* will bring the children, Elders, and the weaker of us to safety?"

Miskinahk stood. "Come forward and announce your intentions, and do so now, because we must be ready."

First out of the crowd came the animals, the pisiskowak, who intended to help the most vulnerable and the very old. Morgan knew this job was as important as any other: the grandparents and the young ones were the future. The grandparents held the future through the stories they had been entrusted with, as Mihko had explained to her. It was their job to not only keep those stories safe within their hearts and minds, but to pass them down to younger generations, so that they would never die. Truly, the only immortal thing in either world was stories. The young ones were the pisiskowak who would grow up to lead Misewa, and who would be given those stories so that one day they could pass them down to others.

Ochek was among the youth in the village, but even still, when all the pisiskowak had come forward that would help guide others to safety, it was Ochek, with his father, who volunteered to fight against Muskwa. Nobody spoke against this, because they knew Ochek was the son of their greatest hunter, and if it was to be his job, one day, to hunt for the village, it was his job, as well, to protect it.

At this point, no one else offered to fight. The other animal beings were waiting to see who else would battle Muskwa. Surely it wouldn't be only Mihko and Ochek.

Arik left the circle and scurried over to Morgan and Eli. She whispered to them, because silence had fallen over the villagers.

"Wow, this is so exciting, right?" Arik said. "I have niska pimples all over my body!"

"Goose," Eli whispered to Morgan.

"Kind of guessed that," Morgan whispered back.

"I mean, who else is going to fight the Great Bear?" Arik asked. "The suspense is killing me. What if it's just those two? Chief Wapistan will be, like, 'I guess my speech wasn't that great,' am I right?"

"They can't beat Muskwa alone. We've seen that." Eli walked away from Morgan and Arik towards the crowd, and put up his hand as though he were in a school classroom.

"I will fight against Muskwa!"

At the sound of his voice, the entire village turned to Eli.

Morgan felt as though there was nothing else she could do. And, as they had discussed, this decision felt like the right decision. The *only* decision.

She stepped forward beside Eli. "I will fight too," she said, although to her own ears her words sounded far less dramatic. She kept picturing herself getting struck in the head by the Great Bear. And, this time, not surviving. It didn't matter, in that moment, that he'd one day be nice and cuddly and sweet, like a teddy bear.

"Me also, I guess," Arik said. Then she added under her breath, "Gotta build up some karma after literally running away last night."

"I like the commitment, Arik," Morgan said.

Remembering their fight with Mahihkan, she knew that Arik was good with a Bo staff. But she also knew that the squirrel wasn't much of a fighter. Then again, neither was Morgan. But Morgan *had* fended off a wolf before. So anybody could do anything if they put their mind to it, even though it was doubtful a burning piece of wood would turn away the Great Bear. And she felt rightly inspired by both Mihko and Wapistan. They'd made her feel ready to face the danger headed their way.

Arik seemed to have stirred something in the gathering. She was a nomad, a visitor to Misewa, somebody who came and went as dictated by the seasons or the availability of food. But there she was, standing up alongside two other visitors to the community—Morgan and Eli—and it must have made residents of Misewa, those who were physically able, feel cowardly and disloyal for not offering to fight Muskwa. Morgan looked out at the crowd. One animal being looked as though she was about to step forward—Casey, the fox—but before she could volunteer, one of the seven Bird Warriors launched out of a tree and landed on the ground. The villagers gasped.

"Stop!"

Pip landed on the ground in what Morgan could only describe as a superhero landing, then stood and looked out over the crowd.

"Stop," he said more quietly. "There will be no more pisiskowak offering their blood to protect this place while the Bird Warriors are here. That is not your role; it is ours. You, all of you, will leave Misewa to our defense, and trust us that there will be a home to come back to."

A hush hung over the crowd like a mist. Morgan waited for somebody, even one animal being, to protest, but none did. Perhaps none dared.

Pip looked up to the trees and called out, "Warriors!"

At the sound of this call, the six remaining birds, one by one, landed on the ground between Chief and Council and the villagers. As each one of the Bird Warriors landed, Arik whispered their name to Morgan.

There was Pip, the robin and leader of the Bird Warriors, his white breast blinding. There was Cee Cee, the duck, her green head glimmering like frost-covered emerald grass in the morning. There was Mickey, the eagle, his enormous wingspan casting a large shadow across the villagers. There was Pick, the blue jay, feathers at the top of his head fashioned into a Mohawk, the black line around his neck painted red with ocher to appear like a necklace of blood. There was Tack, the crane, towering above the others with his long legs. (Morgan could hardly believe that one day it would be Tahtakiw who would betray Misewa.) There was Choch, the blackbird, her orange beak pronounced against a body that looked like a shadow, as though she could come upon you like a nightmare. And finally, there was Chaos, the bittern, lurching forward as though always ready to strike, their crazy eyes piercing, their long beak covered in rusty ocher or dried blood, Morgan couldn't tell which.

Each bird wore a helmet made out of hide, kind of like an old-school football helmet, Morgan thought. A strap crossed their breasts from shoulder to waist, holding a weapon at their back—a sword, or a spear, or a bow and arrow, or an ax. And around every thin ankle was a leather bracelet marked with notches. Morgan would find out later that these weren't notches that counted days. Instead, they were an indication of their effectiveness as warriors, a way to intimidate and ward off those beings who would dare attack Misewa.

Once all seven Bird Warriors had gathered in front of the crowd, they stood in a perfect line. They stared proudly at the villagers, who stared back at them with awe and a bit of fear. But everyone there now also saw hope for the safety of Misewa. For who could ever defeat such fierce soldiers, ready to defend this place at any cost?

Certainly not the Great Bear.

TWENTY-TWO

The Bird Warriors positioned themselves at stations around the perimeter of Misewa, some on the ground, some in the trees, watching for the arrival of Muskwa. The other villagers were in the process of leaving the village. They would set up camp deep in the southern woods and return only when they were fetched, once the battle was over.

In the meantime, Chief and Council invited Mihko, Ochek, Arik, and the siblings inside the Council Hut to discuss whether they could still fight beside the Bird Warriors. There wasn't much of an argument when it came to the involvement of Mihko and Ochek. Mihko had fought to defend Misewa before and, with his son, would fight to defend their home again. The argument concerned the participation of the humans, along with the nomadic, and at times troublesome, Arikwachas.

"You are all strangers to this village, in a manner of speaking," Chief Wapistan said. "Arikwachas, you have come here to stay from time to time, as it has suited you.

Morgan and Eli, you've been with us for weeks, and though your stay has been good, why has it been long enough that you would risk your lives for the beings of Misewa?"

"*Who* would do such a thing?" Oho asked. "Even the nomadic ones that stay here as far back as time recalls left to save themselves when Nikamon brought word of Muskwa."

"And what use is a human anyway, in a battle like this?" asked Miskinahk. "I've never seen one strong or skilled enough, and you are only children."

"So's Ochek," Morgan said. "He's a child, isn't he?"

"Ochek was raised on the land." Oho chuckled. "He was born to it. Is that the Ochek you speak of?"

"Well, yeah . . ." Morgan looked down and dug her toe into the dirt. She couldn't think of anything to say in response. Her argument had fallen flat.

"Chief and Council," Eli said. "I was raised on the land. I was born to it, just like Ochek. I lived there the first years of my life, until just recently, when I was taken away against my will and the will of my family. If that's how you decide who can fight and who can't, then you have to let me do it, and you have to let my sister too. Because the land is in her blood, just like it's in mine."

"Whoa," Morgan whispered to Eli. "Are you taking tips on how to give speeches from Mihko?"

"It feels like speeches work around here," Eli whispered back.

Morgan tried to pick up where Eli had left off. "Chief Wapistan, Oho, Miskinahk. We've lived here with you, even if it's been for just a short time. We've, like, tried to live in a good way, just like you wanted us to. We've gotten to know Misewa and the pisiskowak who live here." She put her arm around Eli. "Eli and I feel like this has become . . . a special place for us. We don't want to see it ruined, and we can help. We know we can."

"You're not so bad either," Eli whispered to her.

"Chief Wapistan and Council, if I may," Arik said. "I also was born to the land . . ."

"Arikwachas," Miskinahk said, "we know you have lived on the land, obviously."

"Yes, don't repeat the humans. They spoke well for themselves," Oho said.

"Well, I *was* born to the land," Arik grumbled. "Anyway, I know that I haven't lived here all the time, but gosh, I'd like to one day. I mean, we could ease into it, you know? I could stay here once in a while, then stick around a little longer. No need to rush things. Maybe first it would just be every other week, and then—"

"Ahem." Chief Wapistan hid a smile, but tried to convey seriousness with his eyes. "Maybe get to the point, Arikwachas. I'm not getting any younger."

"You can call me Arik, Chief," she said. "And let me just say, I've known these two humans for but a day, but I've found them quite fun and very loyal to Askí, the North Country, and Misewa. I feel inspired by them, honored ones. If they want to fight to save this village, then I think I'd like to fight with them, at their side. I mean, at their side and the side of the Bird Warriors and Mihko and Ochek. At *all* the sides, dear Chief and Council. I want to help like I want a nut, you see."

The room fell silent. Outside, aside from shuffling feet as villagers hurried to leave Misewa for the woods, it was quiet. You could almost hear the blades of grass bending underfoot. Silence from anticipation as Chief and Council began to confer, deciding what role the humans and Arik would be allowed to play.

"Good speech too, eh?" Arik whispered to the siblings, offering a break from the tension.

"I mean . . . ," Morgan started.

"Eli?" Arik said.

Eli scrunched his face and tilted his head. "It wasn't *awful*?"

"See? I should've gone first, that's the problem," Arik said. "Following you two. *Really.* Who could do that?"

"You weren't that bad," Morgan assured her. "You were good. It was very . . . Arik . . . of you."

"*Well*"—Arik turned up her snout—"I'm going to take that as a compliment."

At last, Chief Wapistan pushed himself to stand with his cane, took a step forward, and nodded his head weakly. Even the smallest gesture looked as though it took maximum effort.

"We, like Mihko, have had enough of Muskwa pillaging our home without resistance. All we have ever done is retreat, and then, only when safe, return. What more could we do with our village, with our lives, if so much time were not spent running and rebuilding?" Chief Wapistan looked down, and put both paws on the handle of his cane. He closed his eyes. Seeing their Chief struggle, Oho walked over to him, and steadied him.

"Never have we tried to stand up against this threat, this Great Bear. It has seemed an impossible task. Now the village has decided to do just that, and I am proud of their bravery, but I fear even the Bird Warriors won't be enough. I fear Mihko and Ochek won't be enough. And so, we will allow you to join the fight. We thank you for your selflessness in risking your lives to protect our home and the beings within it."

It was decided. And soon the three who had been granted the honor of joining those who would defend Misewa were standing with the Bird Warriors, Mihko, and Ochek. Arik with her trusty Bo staff, Eli with a long spear, Morgan with a slingshot of her construction, and all twelve of them determined to fight Muskwa until the bitter end.

TWENTY-THREE

It was dusk now, and it felt as though it would be dusk forever, as though time had stopped across the North Country. That Askí herself had stopped turning. The twelve warriors who had been tasked with defending Misewa were spread out along the edge of the community that lined the southern woods, watching for the Great Bear to appear. The villagers were now gone from Misewa, hidden safely. At least, if the warriors were to fail, nobody else would get hurt.

Morgan had Eli on her right, several yards away from her, and Arik at the same distance on her left. They were positioned to face southeast. The Bird Warriors and the fishers all faced south and southwest into the forest, where the Great Bear was most likely to come from. As the silence continued, one by one the birds flew to the trees to get a better look. A few even hovered above the trees to watch for a sign of Muskwa's approach: leaves rustling, brush moving, any rumbling sound from the forest. Their wings flapping high above the ground sounded like a distant helicopter.

What kind of a nap is he having? Morgan thought. She imagined him in the middle of a long, leisurely sleep. And why not? He'd just eaten his fill in Otakosík, hadn't he? Morgan always slept well after a big meal. Imagine eating all the food in an entire village. She would never bother to wake up!

Just then, a voice bellowed from above and somewhere to her right.

"He comes!"

All at once, Morgan, Eli, and Arik wheeled around to look in the direction of the voice. High above Misewa was Pick, the blue jay, and he was pointing deep into the woods. Just as though a starter's pistol had been fired, everybody dashed over to the southwest end of the village. They gathered in one tight line, their weapons raised, waiting for the Great Bear to appear.

It was a minute, at most, before Muskwa could be seen stalking through the woods, coming right towards them. At first, the Great Bear didn't even seem to notice them. At first, the Great Bear didn't even look in the direction of the village. He seemed to be strolling through the park, without a care on Askí. He looked to his right, at what, nobody knew. He looked to his left, at something else. Morgan almost imagined Muskwa whistling as he came ever closer, walking on all fours, just a relaxed bear. In fact, Muskwa was less than twenty feet from the perimeter of the village before he finally noticed the twelve beings poised to defend Misewa. And even after he saw the defenders, he just stopped and chuckled. There was no concern on his face, no fear in his eyes. He ended up sitting on the ground and placing his paws on his knees. He looked from left to right at each one of the birds, the fishers, the squirrel, and the humans.

"You're usually all gone by now," he said. "Or at least running away."

"Not this time, Muskwa." Mihko took one step forward. "Not ever again."

Muskwa's chuckle turned to laughter. He grabbed his stomach. He bounced up and down as though the ground were a trampoline. "Says who? You and your weasel son? Two humans? What harm you did to me! What fear you've put in my heart!" And with that gleeful mocking, he laughed even harder.

"You *should* be afraid!" Morgan said.

"That's the thanks I get for letting you live?" he asked.

"Yesterday there weren't twelve of us," Eli said.

"And will the others give you the courage to fight this time, boy? I almost didn't recognize you. I thought you were a sapling before." The Great Bear looked squarely at the Bird Warriors and Arik. "Twelve of you," he scoffed. "You enlisted the help of a bothersome squirrel and seven birds no heavier than a lock of my fur."

Arik gasped. "Who are you calling bothersome?"

"I could use that one's sword"—he pointed towards Pip's weapon—"as a toothpick."

"This toothpick"—Pip unsheathed his sword, which seemed to glow in the dying light—"would carve you into pieces. Turn away, bear, or we'll send you to the Happy Hunting Grounds."

Muskwa roared and stood, showing off, to the twelve gathered against him, his enormous height and strength.

He lunged forward several steps, until he was within ten feet of Misewa's defenders. The Bird Warriors didn't flinch. Mihko and Ochek didn't back down. Neither did Eli or Arik. Morgan's heart was pounding—*thump, thump, thump, thump, thump, thump, thump*—but she, like the others, stood her ground. The Bird Warriors all raised their weapons, and when they did, the other five followed suit. And it was at this time, in this brief moment, that Morgan saw it, like a spark, there and gone. But it had been there, she was certain.

Fear.

"How dare you!" shouted the Great Bear, and the trees quivered at the sound of his voice. He landed on all fours heavily. The thud shook the earth. A cloud of dirt rose into the air. "I will take what I want, and you will not try to stop me!"

"How dare *you*!" Morgan shouted, bolstered by the distress she'd seen in him, however brief it was. "Destroying homes! Hurting people! Stealing from them! And for what? Why? Why would you do that?"

The Great Bear looked taken aback by her, as though she herself had roared. He lost his rage for a moment before finding it. He made a ferocious sound that made the woods shudder. "Are you not afraid of me, Iskwésis?"

Morgan locked eyes with the Great Bear, but she didn't see the bear who was in front of her now. Rather, she saw the Muskwa she knew. The kind bear. The wise bear. The bear who would sit with her just outside of the village, on the Barren Grounds, and look up at the sky with her to stare at Ochek's constellation. The bear who would let her put her head against his chest, and rest there, his fur like the most comfortable blanket. The bear who would put his arm around her, his paw on her shoulder, and do so with great care so as not to burden her with too much weight. At the question of whether or not she was afraid of *this* Great Bear, then, Morgan said simply, "No."

"You will be, little human! I will not make the same mistake!" Muskwa paced back and forth mere feet away from the group of twelve standing shoulder to shoulder. He locked eyes with each of them in turn, trying, Morgan thought, to look as mean as he could.

"You are *all* weak. You're no match for me. Run away, like you've always done! Run away and I'll spare your lives! I may even leave you my scraps!"

"You're right," Mihko said, "we may not be a match for your size and strength. Alone, we are weak." He paused, then looked down the line from left to right. "But together, we are strong. Stronger than even you, Great Bear."

Pip raised his sword over his head. "So come and do your worst, Muskwa. Come, try to take our village again."

"You'll have to get through us first," Ochek said.

The Great Bear roared one last time, and got to his feet. A final attempt to intimidate them, to get the twelve to run away and hide. But not one of them backed away. Not one of them moved. And so there was a standoff. There was no roaring. There were no threats sent either way. Amid the tension, there fell a great silence. It reminded Morgan of a scene from an old western, with the good guy facing the bad guy, each ready to draw his gun on the other. She almost expected a tumbleweed to roll between Muskwa and the twelve warriors. But there was no tumbleweed.

Instead, a cry erupted from the Bird Warriors. They would stand and wait for a battle no longer. They would start it.

Pip rose from the ground, followed by his band of six. They hovered there for just a second before flying towards the Great Bear. Upon seeing this, Mihko, Ochek, Arik, Eli, and Morgan broke into a run just behind the birds. They charged at Muskwa. Muskwa did not charge towards them. He turned and ran the other way. The twelve did not stop. They pursued the Great Bear, because they knew if they did not, he would just come back again at another time, and they were determined that his assaults on Misewa would stop forever.

Muskwa, when behaving in a fearful and cowardly way, was really quite fast. He barreled away from those in pursuit, on all fours, deeper and deeper into the southern woods. The Bird Warriors flew after him, dodging trees expertly, like they were scout troopers on speeder bikes in *Return of the Jedi.* They were quick and nimble. Trailing behind, in order, were Mihko and Ochek, Arik, then the children, a fair distance back but running as fast as they could.

Now, Muskwa was fast, but he'd also just woken from a nap and his belly was still full of the enormous meal he'd enjoyed the night before. So Morgan wasn't surprised to see, in the distance, through the dense southern woods, the Bird Warriors dive towards the ground. They'd finally caught up to the Great Bear.

Morgan and Eli continued to run, especially when they saw that Mihko, Ochek, and Arik had joined the fray. Morgan saw weapons rise, then fall. She saw a bird, then a fisher, get tossed away, then jump right back into the fight.

She heard shouting, cries of pain. She saw Muskwa swipe animal beings away with his thick, long arms. The ground quivered beneath the weight of the battle. And then finally they arrived, just in time to hear the Great Bear roar the loudest roar Morgan had heard from him yet. Pip, Chaos, Mickey, and Pick dive-bombed Muskwa with their weapons, screaming like a flock of banshees. One of them struck into his hide; he cried out in pain. He grabbed Chaos and Mickey out of the air and threw them into Pip and Pick, knocking all four of them away. Tack and Cee Cee hovered over the Great Bear's head and started pecking and clawing around his ears. While he dealt with them, swinging a weapon that had been dropped, Choch stabbed him in the leg. Muskwa's knee buckled, and, with a heavy thump, he hit the ground.

The animal beings and the Bird Warriors took the opportunity presented to them. All at once—leaping, climbing, flying—they swarmed Muskwa. The birds and fishers were all landing blows on the Great Bear.

Morgan and Eli, who'd been standing off to one side watching everything happen, looked at each other, then nodded before charging into the fight and leaping onto the bear along with all the others. Eli hammered down on Muskwa's fur with the shaft of his spear, not willing or able, Morgan thought, to use the sharp end of the weapon. Morgan's slingshot, in this close encounter, was useless. She opted instead to punch her old friend over and over again. Each time her fist landed against his soft fur, she wanted to sob for what she was doing, and she had to keep repeating to herself, *He doesn't die, he doesn't die, he doesn't die*. It almost worked, at least for a short while, during those seconds that all twelve warriors were attacking the bear. But then her punches became something else. They became less about defeating an enemy and more about frustration. Why did he have to be like this? Why was he doing the things that he was doing? Why couldn't he be the way she knew him to be? Why was he making them hurt him?

That's when the tears came. And the tears continued to fall, one drop for every punch, it seemed, until Muskwa, the Great Bear, erupted from the ground and onto his feet, throwing all twelve of Misewa's protectors off him and hurtling across the forest floor. Morgan rolled up to the base of a tree, and looked up at the beast. He was furious, wild with pain, his fur matted with blood, his face swollen.

"I will kill each one of you!" Muskwa shouted.

Ochek was the closest to him. The Great Bear raised his arm to strike the animal being with a terrible blow, one that he might not have survived. *Was this going to change the future?* Morgan thought. *Had they done something wrong?* She scrambled for her slingshot.

"No!"

Eli came sprinting towards the Great Bear just as the beast was about to level his assault on the young hunter. Muskwa was distracted for the briefest moment, but long enough. Eli drove his spear deep into the bear's shoulder. Muskwa put both paws around the spear and pulled the sharp end out of his body, then swung it at Eli, knocking him to the ground.

"Eli!"

Ochek scrambled to safety. The Great Bear readied to hit

Eli again. Eli, who was unconscious. Muskwa had let Morgan live. He was not about to give Eli the same consideration.

As Muskwa raised the spear, with the sharp tip threatening Eli, Morgan lifted her slingshot with desperate speed and pulled back the round stone. She took aim at the Great Bear, her hand steady. Muskwa thrust downward. She released the projectile, and it whipped through the air, straight and true. Just before the spear pierced Eli's skin, the stone struck Muskwa right between the eyes. He was knocked backward, and dropped his weapon. He grabbed at his face with his paws.

Pip exploded from the ground, flew almost above the forest, then plummeted through the air at Muskwa.

"You will kill nobody!"

The leader of the Bird Warriors bellowed a war cry and slashed violently at the Great Bear's chest. There was a flash and then a desperate cry of agony. Blood splashed from the bear onto the ground, the trees, the warriors. Blood painted Pip's white breast red. Muskwa fell to his knees, grasping his chest. He swayed like a single blade of grass in the wind, and then the Great Bear dropped sideways. The ground rumbled one last time as Muskwa connected with the earth.

The Bird Warriors, Mihko, Ochek, and Arik stood in a circle around him, all looking down on the beast. Morgan rushed over to her brother, who was still unconscious, as soon as she knew the battle had ended. She dragged him up onto her lap, placed one arm under his neck, the other across his waist, and cradled him safely in her arms. Then she, too, turned her attention to the Great Bear.

Muskwa writhed on the ground, rocking back and forth, his paws pressed against a gaping wound across his chest. The strike from Pip's sword had opened a large slash for such a small weapon, and it continued to bleed, flowing out from underneath the bear's paws, pooling on the ground beneath the animal being.

The leader of the birds sheathed his sword. "You underestimated what we could do together, as one."

Muskwa coughed, and blood misted from his mouth. "M-maybe I . . . I did. May—maybe I did. You're. Right."

Morgan just stared helplessly at Muskwa, watching him suffer, knowing that, nevertheless, he would live through this. Nobody there would have believed it, but she knew it to be true. That didn't make it easier to witness all the cuts and blows wounding the Great Bear's body. Morgan, who hadn't really stopped crying since she'd inflicted some of those wounds herself, took inventory of every one of the injuries. Especially the cut made by Pip's sword. Then it hit her. This was what had made the scar on Muskwa's chest. A reminder, always, of what had happened on this day.

"What's . . . to risk . . . your lives . . . f-for . . . in Mis . . . Misewa?" the Great Bear asked. "I could've . . . killed you."

"It's not just a village, Muskwa," Pip said. "It's our home. It's a community."

"And if you'd have just asked to stay with us, we would've welcomed you into our home," Choch said.

"But you chose greed," Chaos said.

"You . . . w-wouldn't . . . have welcomed me. You lie." Muskwa looked away from the warriors standing over him.

His eyes settled on Morgan.

"They welcomed me," she said. She ran her hands through Eli's hair. "They welcomed him."

"And they welcomed me," Arik said, "kind of. I showed up and . . . well, a lot was going on. But I'm sure they would've welcomed me. I mean, they have before."

"We will do you one favor, Great Bear," Pip said. "We will ease your suffering." The leader of the Bird Warriors looked to Mihko. "Mihko, the one who is called Blood, this honor falls on you, as it has before."

Mihko nodded. He began to raise his weapon—a spear adorned with feathers and a sharp stone head—but stopped. "No." He lowered his weapon, and handed it to his son. "The time will come when this will be your village to provide for, to help protect. You're not a child any longer, and this is a responsibility I give to you."

"Ehe, Nipapa." Ochek took the spear.

"Please," the Great Bear said.

Ochek raised the weapon, ready to deliver a fatal blow.

"Forgive me," the Great Bear said.

Morgan could see Ochek's paws shaking, gripped so tightly around the spear. Then, he thrust downward.

"No!" Morgan cried.

This wasn't how it was supposed to happen. But the weapon punctured the earth, inches from Muskwa's head. Ochek released it. The shaft wobbled, the feathers swayed from the movement, and the spear was left unattended. The Great Bear had been shown mercy.

TWENTY-FOUR

Nobody questioned why Ochek spared Muskwa, and it was something Ochek never explained. If Ochek was set to be the provider and a protector of Misewa, his decision was one to be respected. But something that Ochek had said to Mahihkan—when the wolf was wounded and at Ochek's mercy—kept repeating in Morgan's mind: *Where's the sport in killing something so wretched?* So defenseless too. There couldn't have been much honor in that. Wretched now, revered later.

It took all seven birds and the animal beings to bring Muskwa to the village; after seeing the weapon narrowly miss his head, the Great Bear had passed out. Morgan carried Eli until he woke up and insisted that he could walk. He had a bad bruise on his hip, but he recovered well and quickly.

Not only had Ochek spared Muskwa's life, but the fisher family volunteered to nurse him back to health. They took him into their longhouse, in the back room, and tended to him there. And care he needed, with the injuries the Great Bear had sustained from all the blows that had landed, the weapons that had struck true, including Eli's spear to the shoulder. Mostly, though, it was the sword wound across Muskwa's chest that had done the most severe damage. The violent slash had opened the Great Bear up like game that had been caught in a snare. Nicky, in particular, busied herself with Muskwa. She, just like the wounded bear, was hardly seen for the first days after the battle, appearing outside of the fishers' longhouse only to gather medicine that was hanging outside the front door, then disappearing back inside.

Life in Misewa soon returned to normal, or as normal as it could be with an enormous injured bear in the bedroom of the fishers' dwelling. The villagers had returned right away, led by Arik, who volunteered to fetch them after the fight was over. The Bird Warriors had flown back up to the trees, maintaining their seemingly endless watch, their work to keep the village safe. And Pip, the leader, never did wash the bear's blood off his breast, and for that reason he looked forevermore like the robin Morgan and Eli were familiar with back on earth. Arik stuck around for the time being as a visitor, and took up residence in Morgan and Eli's teepee, welcomed there heartily and excitedly by the children. The other teepees became occupied again by nomadic animal beings who'd left Misewa upon hearing word that the Great Bear was coming.

A little more than a week later, five weeks into the siblings' stay, Muskwa was well enough to leave the bedroom, and he spent his days sitting in front of the longhouse on an oversized bench that Mihko had constructed for him. He sat quietly and reflectively, watching life go on in the village, watching the community that he had never seen before. None of the villagers spoke to him for those first few days after he ventured outside. They would look at him curiously, warily, but they would leave him be. This was understandable. The bear who had laid waste to Misewa more than once was now sitting on a bench outside a village longhouse. This time as a guest. There was confusion at this, and a lingering fear like embers within a fire, that would take time to die out entirely.

Even the siblings kept their distance from Muskwa at first, until one night, when the sky was crystal clear and the countless stars burned almost as bright as one sun, Morgan approached Muskwa and his custom-made bench. She put a stool down beside him, and sat. They both watched the village, not so much looking at each other, until Morgan cleared her throat and broke the silence. She looked at the healing wound, the angry line across his chest from his shoulder towards his hip.

"Does it hurt?" she asked.

Muskwa looked down at the developing scar. "Only the memory of it now."

"Memories can be hard to carry, depending on what they are."

"Yes."

She put a hand on his shoulder, as though this younger

Muskwa was her Muskwa. "You just need to learn how to carry them in a better way."

"I'm ashamed of what I did," Muskwa admitted. "Of hurting you and your brother. Of causing such destruction for so long. I'm ashamed of all that I did—and for what? I wanted things, so I took them. Never did I think to ask. Never did I want to. I . . . I liked the power."

"Taking things because you're bigger isn't power."

"I know that now. I wonder . . ." He took a moment to look at the villagers moving about, the longhouses and teepees and wigwams humming with life. "I wonder if they'll ever really forgive me."

She patted his shoulder. "Of course they will. Muskwa, I've learned that anything can happen here. You just, I don't know, need to know that they're good people and that good things will happen. Have a bit of faith."

"You almost died, young one, and at my hands. How could you not hate me for that?"

"I almost died? Nah. I got a little bump on the head. At worst, you gave me a minor concussion. A kid in elementary school gave me one of those once when we were playing red rover. I didn't hold that against them either. Plus, you have to get some points for not killing me. You could've just stepped on me or whatever."

"I couldn't," he said, "for some reason."

"Maybe for the same reason Ochek didn't kill you."

"*I* almost died."

"Totally. You *actually* almost died. I mean, if he had . . . well, you know . . . but then just from the blood loss! I mean, wow. You probably lost a *crazy* amount of blood."

"Nikamon provided good care, and good medicine." Muskwa shook his head, and looked to the stars regretfully. "It seems as though everybody gives, and all I've ever done is take."

"People, animal beings, whatever," she said, "they can change. It's never too late."

Muskwa looked away from the stars to Morgan. "Do you think so?"

"I know so," Morgan said. "Trust me. You'll be okay. Everything will be. Just because one thing happened before, it doesn't mean a different thing can't happen in the future."

Right then, for a split second then gone, Morgan thought of her mother. Jenny Trout.

"Maybe you're right, little one." He put a paw atop Morgan's hand, and patted it gently. "I hope that when I die, it's while doing something as selfless and brave as you twelve warriors."

"That's a choice you have to make."

"I think it's a choice I've made already," the Great Bear said.

TWENTY-FIVE

The next three weeks passed quickly, with no regard for how badly Eli and Morgan wanted to stay. Ochek was a part of their lives again, living and breathing, just as they'd hoped he would be. They had Ochek, young or old. They had Arik, who'd decided to stick around for as long as Morgan and Eli planned on staying. They had Muskwa, who, day by day, came out of his shell, began to speak to villagers, and eventually moved from that custom-made bench to help out around Misewa. They had everything, so when the time came for the siblings to leave, even though it had been eight weeks, it felt as though it had been only eight hours.

Misewa Math in reverse.

On the night Morgan and Eli were to depart, Misewa held a feast for them. All the villagers, all the visitors, gathered in the circle in front of the Council Hut. All the animal beings and the two humans sat on the grass together during a particularly beautiful and clear autumn evening, surrounding the blanket holding the food.

It was a rather subdued gathering. The children had told the villagers that they would not be back, that they would never see the villagers again, that they would not return to Misewa. And because they had become a part of the community, it was, in the end, a sad occasion. Of course, Morgan and Eli *would* be back, they knew that, but they'd remained loyal to the promise they had made. They would not tell any of the animal beings what lay ahead, and that included their role in the future. What was to happen had to happen. They were as certain of this as they'd been that they had to help defend Misewa against Muskwa. They were always going to travel back in time to do what they did. They'd come for Ochek, but it turned out that their journey had ended up being for so much more.

Morgan and Eli left after the feast ended. Their departure was made easier to tolerate when both Arik and Ochek offered to walk them across the Barren Grounds. It allowed the siblings to delay what they both knew would be an incredibly hard act: leaving Ochek to the past. Doing so would be like seeing him die all over again, and if they didn't have to say goodbye right away, they were happy not to. They walked slowly across the empty plains, sometimes talking with Ochek and Arik and other times just walking quietly, side by side, savoring the time they had with the young fisher. Morgan tried her best to will the Great Tree not to appear, for the northern woods lined up across the horizon not to come into view, wishing their walk could last forever, then longer. But sadly, unavoidably, the time came when they arrived at their destination.

"Well . . ." Morgan couldn't stand to look at the Great Tree until absolutely necessary. She had her back to it, opting to pay full attention to Arik and Ochek. "I guess this is it, huh?"

Her intention to play it cool went out the window, and she rushed towards Ochek and gathered him in her arms. She even lifted the animal being off his feet and twirled him around once. Ochek and Morgan were soon joined by Eli, the two humans sandwiching the young fisher. Not wanting to be left out, Arik grabbed on as well, and there they were, spinning around in a four-person embrace, desperate to hang on for as long as they could.

Much too soon, however, Eli tugged at Morgan's sleeve, and the rotating hug came to a stop slowly, like the end of a ride at a carnival. They were positioned like so: Morgan facing the Barren Grounds, Ochek facing the mountains to the west, Arik facing whatever lay to the east, and Eli facing the Great Tree.

"What is it?" Morgan asked her brother. His face carried a look of grave concern.

They let go of one another, and Morgan turned around. She saw then what Eli had seen. The boards they'd hammered over the portal that led into their secret room had been broken away from the Great Tree. They lay in shattered pieces on the ground at its roots.

"Oh no," Morgan whispered.

She hurried over to inspect the boards. Eli was immediately beside his sister, and together they inspected the damage as though they were investigators at an accident scene. They looked inside the portal to find the door to their secret room closed. They looked at the nails, most still hammered into the tree. That's when Morgan saw it. And she gasped loudly, because she knew at once who had come through the portal. There was a piece of ripped fabric stuck to the head of one of the nails. It was blue, just like the color of Mason's overalls, the ones that looked like work pants.

"These are his," Morgan said.

"They have to be," Eli agreed.

"*He's* renovating Katie and James's attic!" Morgan cried.

She tore the fabric off the nail. It all made sense. To get to Askí, he would have had to come through the portal. Morgan had always wondered how he'd arrived, since the portal was in their attic. Had he been a burglar who'd broken into their house long before Morgan and Eli came to live there? Had he owned the house before Katie and James? No, he'd been a worker, hired to renovate the attic. A bad worker, who showed up only rarely. It so happened that he'd decided to work on the attic on the day that Morgan and Eli stayed home from school, when they'd pretended to be sick. It so happened that he'd come to work on the day, the only day, that the siblings had opened the portal in daylight, and into the past. An enormous weight fell on Morgan's shoulders.

"It's our fault," she whispered.

"What's our fault?" Eli asked.

"All of it," she said. "The White Time, everything that happened because of it. He's here now, and he's here because of us. We had to help save the North Country because it's our fault that everybody almost died."

"The White Time?" Ochek asked.

Clearly, he and Arik had been listening with interest to everything Morgan and Eli had said.

"I was more concerned with the part about almost everybody dying, myself," Arik said.

"Yeah, that wasn't great," Ochek said. "But the White Time comes once a year, and we know how to live through it."

"Look," Morgan said. "There's something you both need to know. We"—Morgan pointed to herself and Eli—"we . . . well, this isn't the first time we've been to—"

"Morgan!" Eli interrupted.

"We *have* to tell them now. I think . . . I think we've always had to tell them, at least something. At least enough."

"What? Why?"

"Don't you get it? The very first time we came here, when Ochek told us about the humans who'd been here before us, when Arik told us . . ." She paused to see if Eli would have the revelation she'd just had, but when he didn't follow her, or was too shocked to respond, she continued. "When Arik told us about those same humans, that was *us*, Eli. They were talking about us."

"But we haven't told them . . ." Eli then had the revelation. His head tilted back, and he slapped himself on the forehead for not getting it sooner. "We're going to tell them now."

"This whole time we were wondering who those humans could've been, and it was us all along!"

""Ummm"—Ochek leaned in so that his head was between Morgan and Eli—"sorry, but what are you two talking about?"

"We've been here before, to Misewa," Morgan said. "To Askí. But, we've been here, like, in the future."

"*What?*" Arik put her paws on her hips. "What are you going on about? In all my years, I've never—"

"There's a first time for everything," Eli said.

"There are things we need to tell you," Morgan said to the animal beings, "and there are things we can't tell you, even if we know it might help, because what happens needs to happen."

"Okay, I'm lost," Ochek said.

"Something bad is going to happen here," Morgan said. "We don't know when, but we four together, we'll be the ones to make things right. Do you trust me?"

"Ehe," Ochek said. "I do."

"Me too," Arik said. "Who'd make up something like this?"

They decided to split up, far enough that one pair couldn't hear what the other was saying, because Morgan and Eli agreed that Ochek and Arik had been told different things about the future. Ochek, for example, knew to find the children at the Great Tree. Arik, meanwhile, knew where the summer birds were. Knowing Ochek, if Morgan were to tell him where the summer birds would be kept, there was no way he would wait for Morgan and Eli and Arik. He'd go off on his own right away and probably die. It would be noble, but Misewa would lose its best hunter and the village would eventually starve. The only thing she decided to tell Ochek was what she knew, without a doubt, he had been told by, well, her.

"So," Morgan said when she was alone with Ochek, "it's very simple. Like I said, something bad is going to happen, and it's not going to go away for a long time. So long that you're going to count the days with notches. They're going to be all over the walls in your longhouse."

"Why would I ruin my house like that? My dad would kill me!"

"Well, you do. Trust me. Anyway, there'll come a time when there are almost no spaces left on the wood for any more notches. When that time comes, you need to come out here, every day, until Eli and I come back. First Eli, then, a couple of weeks later, me."

"You're going to come back? But you said—"

"I know what we said, but we couldn't tell the others about this, and *you* can't either. In fact, when we come back, years from now, they have to act as though they've never met us before. Nothing can be changed. Promise?"

"Yes." Ochek nodded. "You have my word. They will not greet you. They will not welcome you. You will be like strangers to them." He paused, then added reluctantly, "And to me."

"Pinkie swear?"

"What's a—?"

"You just go like this." Morgan stuck out her pinkie, then she got Ochek to stick out what amounted to his pinkie on his paw, and they curled them around each other. "There. Now we've made the best promise ever that you can't break, and neither can I. Got it?"

"That was really weird but, yes, I got it."

"Good."

Morgan hugged Ochek again, and didn't let go until she saw that Arik and Eli had finished their talk. Morgan would find out later how Eli had explained everything that was necessary for Arik to know. How one day, many years from now, she would be living on the land, off traps set by Ochek, on the trapline he would inherit from his father. She would be eating a hare out of a trap when he and Morgan would return, accompanied by Ochek. Ochek would want to eat her, despite knowing her, and the only way she could save her own life would be to tell him where a treasure was being held (he did not tell her that it was the summer birds). Over the mountains, directly west from the sequoia, on a tiny island, in a cabin. All four of them would have to go to find the treasure.

"What kind of treasure could be so precious?" Arik asked.

"You'll know exactly what kind of treasure when it's time," Eli said cryptically.

"Oh, I adore mysteries!" Arik said.

The two pairs came back together at the entrance to the secret room, at the base of the Great Tree.

"I guess this is it," Morgan said. "For real."

She helped Eli climb through the portal, then Ochek helped Morgan. As he eased her down into their secret room, she held on to his paw for longer than she needed to.

"I'm going to miss you so much."

Tears streamed down her cheeks. She was grateful to have seen him again. It was a blessing that she would never forget. But she knew, at the same time, that she couldn't stand to go back into the past and see him once more. Because in that moment, it hurt far too much to say goodbye, just as much as when he was placed among the stars.

"I'll miss you too, Morgan," Ochek said. "But we'll see each other again if your crazy story is true!"

"Yeah." He was right. He would see her again. But she would not see him. "We will."

Next, Eli said his goodbye to Ochek, which was just as weepy as Morgan's goodbye had been. Then, in true Arik style, she shoved her head through the portal, pushing Ochek out of the way. It brought much-needed levity.

"The time will be a drop in the bucket for an old fart like me," Arik said.

Arik was right, it would be tomorrow when Morgan and Eli saw her again. But present-day Arik would have been waiting over a year for them by the time they got back to Misewa. How much would Misewa have changed, if not the timeless squirrel herself?

"See you, Arik," Morgan said.

"Ekosani, for everything," Eli said.

At that moment, through the door to their secret room, all the way from the first floor, Morgan heard the quick, successive beeps that meant somebody had opened the front door. Somebody had come home from work. Probably Katie. The first thing she would do was check on her and Eli. They had to be in bed, fast, or else they'd be caught.

"We have to go!"

Morgan took a last look at Ochek, then pulled the paper away from the wall. She didn't even hold on to Eli's drawing after the portal had closed. It fluttered downward, and the siblings were probably in bed before it even hit the ground, just before Katie got to the second floor.

TWENTY-SIX

Katie and James came home at the same time, so they could see the kids together, they said. It was the first time either Morgan or Eli had been "sick," and as they were Katie and James's first kids, Morgan figured the foster parents had likely been freaking out a little bit. (She later discovered seventeen missed calls and messages on her phone.) It was a miracle they'd not come home during the day to check on the siblings.

Morgan listened while her foster parents visited Eli. She was sure that Eli was doing what they'd planned to do while racing down the stairs from the attic—pretending to sleep, with the covers pulled up to his chin—because neither of them had had time to take off their new, Nicky-made Misewa clothes. These were mementos from their trip to the past that Morgan was sure they'd wear to Askí on each and every trip from now on—a small way to remember all the relatives they'd spent time with, and, of course, young Ochek. But what explanation could there possibly be if their foster parents saw them wearing the clothing? That while they were sick they'd decided to dress up like characters from Robin Hood? Who cosplayed when they were too sick to go to school?

"Shhh," Katie said. "He's sleeping."

"Feel his forehead," James said.

Morgan heard three soft footsteps, then waited.

"He's clammy," Katie announced.

"Is his hair shorter?" James asked.

Morgan began to subconsciously chew at the edge of her covers, as though they were fingernails. Eli's hair! He must not have put his hood up. It had grown over the eight weeks they'd spent in Misewa, especially with the help of Ochek's fish oil, but had it grown long enough to fool Katie and James? Morgan hoped that enough of Eli's high ponytail was hidden between his head and his pillow. Otherwise her only option was to distract their foster parents somehow, maybe cough violently and lead them away from Eli.

It was quiet for too long. If it were any more tense, Morgan thought she might chew up her entire comforter.

"I don't know," Katie said. "It's hard to tell."

"Should we wake him up and find out?" James asked. "Or is it normal if he cut it?"

"I think we need to learn when we should get involved and when we shouldn't." Katie was very measured. "Let's let him bring it up, if he wants." There was a pause. "It's not that much shorter, if at all, really."

Morgan thought Katie must have been taking a longer look at Eli's hair.

"So we just let him sleep?" James asked.

“Yes,” Katie said.

Morgan, for more than one reason, felt a wave of relief. They weren’t going to question Eli about his hair after noticing a change, however slight it appeared, and according to Katie his forehead felt clammy. That meant it felt sick.

In their hurry, there’d been no time to fake their illness—rub their faces vigorously to look flushed, put a bit of dark eye shadow under their eyes to create the appearance of bags, place their foreheads near a light bulb to conjure up the illusion of a fever. Luckily, they’d just come from a cool North Country evening, had just finished crying, and had just run from their secret room to their bedrooms. All that contributed to what Katie had found in touching Eli’s forehead.

The next thing Morgan heard were footsteps leading from Eli’s bedroom towards hers. Stupidly, thinking too much again, and worrying too much as well, Morgan forgot to pretend she was asleep. Still, as with Eli, everything else was right for her to look and feel sick; she’d confirmed that her skin was clammy, and she had the sheets pulled up to her chin. When Katie and James stopped at the foot of her bed, she nodded weakly to greet them, and coughed once, just enough to not seem forced.

“How are you feeling?” Katie asked.

“Okay, I guess.” She tried to sound croaky. She thought croaky would work in this situation. Croaky went well with clammy.

“Your . . . Katie said that she kept trying to get ahold of you,” James said.

“Oh, really? I’m sorry, I must’ve been sleeping.”

"I figured," Katie said. "It's okay. I managed to hold it together."

"Good job." Morgan maintained the croaky voice facade.

This time, it was James who came forward. He walked around the bed to Morgan's side. He leaned over, and placed the back of his hand against her forehead. He held his hand there for a moment before straightening up. He looked at Morgan as though he knew something or he was figuring something out, and Morgan's heart started to pound. What could he know just from touching her forehead? What kind of a doctor was he? *Thump, thump, thump, thump, thump, thump, thump.* Then he looked at Katie and smiled apologetically, like he'd just lost somebody on the operating table and had to tell the family.

"In my expert medical opinion . . . she'll live."

"Ha, ha," Katie said dryly.

"Wow, a doctor joke," Morgan said. "We've reached a new level in our relationship."

Katie and James smiled, and Morgan smiled an exaggerated sickly smile back.

"If you're hungry, come down for some soup later," Katie said.

"Until then, my prescription is sleep," James added.

"You were doing good," Morgan said. "Don't push it."

"Morgan," Katie said, "did you just meet this guy?"

Morgan listened to them leave and go downstairs to the kitchen. When she was safely alone, she turned on her side and picked up her phone. First, she scrolled through the concerned messages Katie had sent. Next, she listened to the equally concerned voicemails Katie had left. Finally, she went into her contacts and found Jenny Trout. She clicked on Jenny's name. Her thumb hovered over her mother's phone number, and then, as though acting on its own, without giving Morgan any warning, her thumb pressed the number. Morgan's heart started to pound again, and only settled when she quickly hung up before her mother could answer.

Morgan and Eli were not permitted to leave their bedrooms for the rest of the night, except to come down for soup. Morgan was nowhere near hungry after the feast Misewa had hosted for her and Eli, but she went downstairs just to get out of her room.

And of course Katie and James didn't want them going up to their secret room. James even sat at the bottom of the stairs leading up to the attic and worked there deep into the night. But he didn't need to. The siblings had no intention of going to the attic. Not that night. They had accepted, since leaving Misewa in the past, that they wouldn't be able to return to *their* Misewa until the following evening. So, while James worked at the bottom of the stairs, Morgan happily fell asleep before midnight, and did so without even trying to figure out how long they would have been away from the North Country upon their return. She knew Arik would be there, and the rest of their family too.

TWENTY-SEVEN

In the morning, Morgan and Eli didn't act sick at all, didn't care if Katie or James thought it was weird that they'd been ill for only a day. And really, their foster parents seemed more intent on biting their tongues about Eli's hair. He'd put a beanie on as soon as he woke up to hide it from his foster parents and kids at school. The beanie may have covered his head but for sure piqued Katie and James's curiosity. To their credit, however, they didn't ask him about it, no matter how much they may have wanted to. The siblings ate a breakfast of eggs and bacon and sliced oranges and hash browns and toast. Then they walked to school quickly, since Eli didn't have a big drawing pad to slow him.

Morgan walked Eli to his locker first, made sure he was settled, and then walked all the way back to her own. Emily and Morgan talked at their lockers, talked between classes, and sat together for each of their morning classes. One of those classes was Art, where Morgan got Eli another oversized drawing pad. At one point, Morgan explained to Emily why she'd missed school the day before, and kept up the ruse that both she and Eli had fallen ill at exactly the same time. Emily didn't seem to buy it. She had heard about their run-in with the bullies. It had been the talk of the school the day before.

"That's why you didn't come to school yesterday, isn't it?" Emily asked.

It kind of was. Eli had been terrified of the group of five. Morgan had been scared of them too, only acting like she wasn't because she'd promised to protect Eli. They hadn't talked much about them today, but they were on Morgan's mind, and they had to have been on Eli's mind too. Admittedly, if they hadn't gone to Misewa, if time travel hadn't worked, they might have stayed home to avoid another encounter with the bullies. But following their journey to Askí, where they'd met the younger Ochek and stood with the seven Warrior Birds and three animal beings against the Great Bear, there was no fear anymore.

"Yeah," Morgan said. "That's why."

"Just stand up to them," Emily said. "Nobody does. They'd be shocked. Bullies are—"

"Cowards, I know."

"And don't lie to me, okay?"

"I won't. I'm sorry."

Morgan, Eli, and Emily ate lunch together in the gym, at the table where Morgan and Emily always sat. Eli drew in his new drawing pad while Morgan and Emily ate and talked. In Math, they multitasked, texting each other while figuring out algebra, sometimes texting each other precisely *to* figure out algebra. In English, they watched a movie Mrs. Edwards had selected: *Shakespeare in Love.* Emily told Morgan that she loved the film, and so they did not talk at all during class. Then, as quickly as the day had begun, the bell rang and the day was over. Morgan and Emily put away their books and binders, put on their fall jackets and backpacks, and parted ways, since Emily left through a different door than Morgan and Eli.

Morgan met Eli on the stairs in front of the school. Eli had his fall jacket on and his beanie. He was hugging the drawing pad between his arms and chest with a Kung-Fu Grip, just in case. They turned onto the sidewalk, and as they started to walk home, Morgan felt cool concrete on the ball of one foot.

"Hold up a sec," she said.

Eli stopped. Morgan bent over and balanced on one foot while looking at the bottom of the other. Sure enough, she'd worn a hole through her moccasin. It was probably inevitable with all the walking she'd done through the North Country. But how was she going to explain this to Katie?

"Just tell her that they weren't made well?" Eli offered.

"But they *are* made well," Morgan said. "I've walked, like, a thousand miles in these things."

She ran her thumb along the small opening in the sole of the footwear. It was her bony feet, she decided, not the quality of the moccasins. It was why her jeans always ripped at the knees so fast. The "natural" rips Emily liked so much. She was just bony. Bony knees, bony elbows, bony feet. Bony feet and, yes, the incredible amount of walking she'd done.

"Any ideas?"

Eli crouched down and inspected the hole.

"I mean," he said while running his thumb along it just as Morgan had done, "you could get one of the Elders in Misewa to make an exact replica."

Morgan put her foot down and stood up straight. Eli did the same.

"Eli, you're a genius!"

"No, I'm not," Eli said sheepishly. "I just know that, you know, I've been wearing the same moccasins all this time and *they* were made in Misewa, so if they made you a pair, they'd last super long, and Katie and James wouldn't even notice the difference."

"And"—Morgan started to pace—"if I get them to make me a pair the first day we get there, by the time we leave, they'll look all worn-in like this pair is!"

"Exactly."

"I was wrong, brother. *We* are geniuses."

"I'll accept that answer."

"I cannot *wait* for tonight!"

"What if James won't let us up there again?"

"Look." They started walking again. Morgan put her hand on top of Eli's head and made a ruffling motion, as though his hair weren't covered with the beanie. "We're *going* to Misewa tonight, okay? Even if we have to put sleeping pills in James's food, we—"

"Hey!" a familiar voice bellowed behind them. "It's the sisters!"

Morgan looked back. The leader of the bullies was walking close behind them, and his crew was with him, two to a side.

"Leave us alone, would you?" she said.

"I would, but the thing is, I used up all that paper yesterday," he said, "and now I need more. I see your little sister went and got some for me."

Morgan sped up her pace. She took Eli's hand and made him walk as fast as her. If they had to run, then they would run.

"We'll just keep following you until I get what I want," the leader warned. "You might as well just give it to me."

"Just keep walking," Morgan whispered to Eli.

But Eli stopped so quickly that the gang of five almost stumbled over each other.

"No." He turned to face the leader. "You can't have this." Eli held the drawing pad even tighter against his chest. "It's mine."

Eli had his chin up. His chest was puffed out and shielded with the drawing pad, as though it were armor. Morgan took one look at him, then she stood just as tall and strong.

"What's this?" the leader asked. "You guys really think you're going to stop me?"

He reached for the drawing pad, but Eli slapped his hand away. The leader grabbed his own hand with a look of shock on his face, and maybe something else. Maybe, for the briefest moment, fear.

"Give me that drawing pad, little girl. Now."

"Not this time." Eli took a step towards him. "Not ever again."

Morgan moved closer, along with Eli.

The leader stood as tall as he could. A shadow fell across the siblings. He looked squarely at Eli's hand, the one that had slapped his own hand away.

"Says who? You two girls? You're both like toothpicks. I'll break you in half."

"This toothpick"—Morgan put her arm around her brother—"could kick the living crap out of you if he wanted to. Just go away, *jerk*, or he'll show you."

The leader lunged forward with a fist raised, and swung it at Eli. It came within inches of his face, but Eli didn't flinch. He did not back down. Morgan's heart was pounding—*thump, thump, thump, thump, thump, thump, thump*—but she, too, held her ground.

They stood together, united.

"Who do you two think you are?!" shouted the leader. "I'm going to take that drawing pad, and there's nothing you can do about it! There's five of us! There's two of you! Do the math!"

"Actually, there's more." Emily appeared out of nowhere beside Morgan, and took her hand. "You big douche canoe."

Now there were three of them standing strongly together, facing the bullies.

By this time, other kids had gathered around to watch the show. Some were filming the scene. Most of them just stared in awe. Something like this had never happened before.

"I'd do the math," Morgan said, "but I was never really good at it."

And then the most amazing thing happened. The kids who were watching joined with Morgan, Eli, and Emily. One after the other, they came to stand beside them, each one holding the hand of the next. They made a growing line of defense. For Eli, of course, but Morgan couldn't help but think it was for all of them, so that these five wouldn't dare try to take something from, or hurt, any other kids.

The leader began to walk back and forth frantically along the line. This, to Morgan, looked more like panic than an act of intimidation. Still, he looked angry. Afraid and angry.

"You're all going to regret this. You're weak!"

Morgan looked to her left, then she looked to her right. There were twelve of them. But when she looked behind, there were way more than that standing with her and Eli. Too many to count. Thirty, maybe more. She locked eyes with the leader of the gang of bullies.

"Maybe you're right. Alone, we're weak. You could beat one of us up. But you can't beat all of us up, not when we're together. We're stronger than you, you big jerk."

"And you can't have my book!" Eli said in the loudest voice that Morgan had ever heard from him.

The leader shouted an expletive that shouldn't be repeated, a final attempt to intimidate and disband the large group of students. Not one kid backed away; not one of them moved even one step. A few of them just laughed at the leader of the bullies. Was that all he had left? To swear at them?

When the laughter had died down, the group of five bullies stood there, dumbfounded, confused, unsure of what to do. They faced a crowd that had grown to well over fifty students now. Nobody made a sound. Nobody moved. Not until Eli sprang forward with one first raised, as though to punch the leader. The hulking boy, once frightening enough to make Eli cut his braid off, flinched and stumbled, then fell right on his butt. The four others helped him to his feet, and they ran off. The large gathering erupted into cheers, as though their team had just scored to win the championship in overtime.

"See?" Emily said to Morgan over the roar of the crowd. "Bullies are cowards."

Morgan couldn't think of anything else to do or say but hug Emily, right in the middle of the crowd of raucous students, an embrace that was soon joined by Eli, then what felt like a million other kids.

The bullies had been defeated, the drawing pad was in Eli's possession, and tonight they would celebrate by going to Misewa and seeing their friends, their family, who had been waiting for Morgan and Eli for far too long.

TWENTY-EIGHT

That night, Morgan and Eli waited in their bedrooms for Katie and James to go to bed so they could get up, go to the attic, and enter through the portal into the North Country. Morgan could hear Eli's pencil scratching away at a piece of paper in his new drawing pad. She could hear in those pencil strokes excitement and passion. As soon as they'd left the crowd to walk home, Eli had seemed like a new kid, free from the weight that had been on his shoulders.

For her own part, Morgan was imagining how it would go tonight when they climbed through the portal. Would Arik be camped out, waiting for them? Would they cross the Barren Grounds alone and find her in Misewa? Would she appear despondent at first, worried that her human family might never return? Would her eyes then light up at the sight of them? The family she'd not seen for so long had finally come back!

Family.

Morgan pictured Jenny Trout. Her mother. The family she'd not seen since she was a toddler. Since, if her dreams were accurate, she had been ripped from her mother's arms and taken away against her mother's wishes. What would happen if she found the courage to call her mother, and talk to her? What would happen if she visited her? Would she appear despondent, remembering that one day, years ago, she'd lost her daughter? And would her eyes light up at the sight of her?

"But I do have the courage," Morgan whispered. "Look at everything we've done."

She'd been thinking about all these things while staring at the white ceiling, her head resting against her pillow, her hands interlocked behind her head. She'd cast all her thoughts, everything she'd pictured, onto the white walls as though they were a movie screen. But now she turned away from the ceiling and onto her side. She reached to the floor and picked up her phone. She went into her contacts, found the name of her mother, and clicked on her profile. There were her initials: J.T. There was her phone number. Without hesitation, mustering up all the courage she knew she had, Morgan pressed the number with her thumb and put the phone to her ear. She listened to the ringing. Then, the ringing stopped.

"*Tansi*?" a woman's voice said.

"*Tansi*," Morgan said. "I'm looking for my . . . I mean . . . is this Jenny Trout? Is Jenny there?"

"Oh," the woman's voice said. "No. No, Jenny's not here. She, uhhh . . . this is her mother. She—"

"Her mother?" Morgan repeated excitedly. *Oh my god!* she thought. She couldn't believe it. She was talking to her grandmother. Her *kókom*! She'd called to speak to her mother, to one day, maybe, bring their little family together again. But she'd never considered that bringing their family together meant bringing all the relatives she'd never met before into that family. People like her *kókom*. Morgan felt like crying tears of joy. It was happening. This was happening. "You're my—"

"I'm sorry, dear," Morgan's *kókom* said. "Jenny's not here. She . . ." Her voice was breaking. "My daughter is dead."

"What? No. No, that's not right. That can't be, I . . ."

Suddenly, tears of joy turned into something else entirely. Morgan didn't hang up the phone. She just let it go, and it crashed against the bedroom floor. She started to sob uncontrollably. She hugged her knees into her chest. She stared out the window at the streetlight, but she couldn't see the light. There was no light anymore. There was only darkness.

All her life she'd told people that she didn't have a mother, because what kind of mother would have given her daughter away? Now she knew that wasn't the case: she knew that she'd not been given away—but she didn't have a mother, all the same. Her mother was somewhere in the darkness. And so was Morgan.

It could have been minutes later; it could have been hours. Morgan didn't know. She never wanted to see her phone again, as though all of this was her phone's fault. At some point, Eli came into her room. She heard his footsteps.

She hadn't moved. She was still staring out the window, at the streetlight. She was still crying. Her pillowcase was wet with her tears. She was still curled up into a ball.

"Hey," Eli said. "Ready to go?"

He couldn't see that she was crying.

"No." Morgan did her best to keep her voice even. "I'm not going tonight."

"What? Why not?"

"Because I'm tired, Eli. We can go tomorrow night. We were just there."

"Yeah, but not *there* there. Wouldn't it be nice to—?"

"No, it wouldn't be nice. I said I don't want to go." Morgan tried to catch her breath. She started to sob again. Her voice had cracked. Had he noticed?

It was quiet. He was standing at the foot of her bed. She could just imagine him looking at her. Confused. Curious. They'd both desperately wanted to go, and now, suddenly, she didn't. She didn't blame him if he was confused. She didn't blame him if he was curious.

"Well . . . ," he said, "can I go? Just this once?"

"You know we agreed that we wouldn't go alone," she said. "It has to be both of us. You can wait, can't you? It's just a day. Can't you just wait?"

It was quiet again before Eli said, "Yeah, I can wait. Okay."

"Okay. Good night."

Morgan felt bad for being short with him. She felt bad for being so short that she may as well have been snapping at him the whole time. He'd not done anything wrong. When her heart didn't hurt as much, she would apologize. Right now, she wanted to be alone. She heard his footsteps. He left her bedroom, crossed the hallway, entered his own bedroom, and then she heard him lie down on his bed.

Morgan waited for a long time. She waited until she was sure Katie and James were sleeping. She waited until she was sure that Eli was sleeping. Then she got out of her bed and tiptoed all the way to Eli's bedroom, right up to his bedside. By the streetlight, by the moonlight, she flipped open his drawing pad and found the picture he'd been working on. It was just like so many of the ones he'd drawn before. Looking out from the Great Tree, over the Barren Grounds, towards a waiting Misewa. Waiting, just like Morgan. Waiting for somebody who would never come.

She tore the illustration out of the drawing pad, keeping an eye on Eli the whole time to see if she had woken him. She hadn't. She took the drawing with her all the way to their secret room. She stapled it to the wall, corner by corner, and when the last staple had been punched into the wood, the portal opened. She climbed through the opening and left the earth behind.

EPILOGUE

Morgan stood at the base of the Great Tree, its roots beneath her feet. It was nighttime in the North Country, and brilliant starlight was shining down over her body. A light she could not, or would not, see. She stared across the Barren Grounds towards Misewa. She could walk there in the dark. She knew the way. She could wake Arik up. Arik might be able to push some of this pain away with her ceaseless joy. But Morgan kept her feet firmly planted on the roots of the Great Tree. Arik would still be waiting for her tomorrow. Arik would not stop waiting for her, Morgan was certain of that.

She looked away from where she knew Misewa was, and looked up. There, she found the only light she cared to see. Ochekatchakosuk. She kept her eyes on the constellation as she lowered herself to the ground and lay down right on top of the roots, as though she was strong like them. As though they would make her strong enough to get through this.

At some point, Eli climbed through the portal. He must have woken up, or maybe he hadn't been sleeping at all. He didn't say anything to her. He didn't get mad at her. He didn't say anything about her being in the North Country. About her going without him, something they were not supposed to do. He just lay down on the roots of the Great Tree near her, close enough that the tops of their heads were touching. Her feet were pointing west; his feet were pointing east. She slid her hand over the roots towards him. He slid his hand over the roots towards her.

They fell asleep.

Morgan hadn't noticed when she'd arrived, but when she woke up, it was apparent that she'd come to the North Country during the Dying Season. Her entire body was shaking from a chill in the air. Her lips were trembling. She blinked her eyes open to find her eyelashes were frosted, along with every blade of grass that surrounded the Great Tree. She could see her breath. It wafted into the air like a cloud in what was otherwise a perfectly clear morning. She was still holding Eli's hand. She squeezed it.

"Hey, we should go," Morgan said. "It's probably tomorrow morning on earth. Come on, brother."

Eli didn't stir.

"Kid," Morgan said, knowing Eli didn't like to be called that and hoping it would jolt him awake. It didn't. "Katie and James might be up soon if they're not already. Get up!" Again, nothing. Morgan let go of his hand, pushed herself into a sitting position, and nudged Eli's shoulder. He didn't move. He didn't even moan.

"Eli! Wake up! We have to go, like, now."

Nothing. Finally, she rolled him over onto his back. Just how tired was he? When Morgan saw her brother's face, she gasped. His eyes were wide open. For a horrible moment, she thought he was dead, but his hand had not been cold. She checked his pulse, and his heart was beating. She put her ear right close to his mouth, just to be sure, and felt his breath against her skin.

"Eli!"

Morgan shook him violently, but he just lay there, motionless. She reached forward and shut his eyelids, the way they did in movies to people who'd actually died. His eyes must have been super dry. She sat with her back against the Great Tree and looked at him from head to toe, dumbfounded, until she looked beyond his feet at the ground, with all that frosted grass. There were footprints leading to, then away from, where they had slept. She jumped to her feet, and ran over to them. She got down on her knees and placed her hand in one of the footprints. Whatever had come, it was enormous. So much bigger than the Great Bear. She could fit three of her hands in the footprint, easily. What could have made a footprint so big, if not a bear?

"What's bigger than Muskwa in the North Country?" she whispered.

And then she knew. She'd been told the story before by Ochek. One day, a group of villagers had crossed the Barren Grounds so they could hunt in the northern woods. Before entering the forest, they'd rested at the Great Tree. At some point in the night, the same thing that had come to where Morgan and Eli had slept had come into the villagers' teepee. It took the soul of the Elder, Kihiw. Now, it had taken Eli's soul, and left behind only flesh and bones. The name of the thing echoed in Morgan's mind over and over again like a pounding heartbeat.

Mistapew, Mistapew, Mistapew, Mistapew, Mistapew, Mistapew, Mistapew.

The giant had come, and Morgan knew there was only one thing she could do. Enter the northern woods and take back Eli's soul.

DAVID A. ROBERTSON is the author of numerous books for young readers including *On the Trapline*, which won the 2021 Governor General's Literary Award and *When We Were Alone*, which also won the Governor General's Literary Award. *The Barren Grounds*, the first book in the middle-grade The Misewa Saga series, received a starred review from *Kirkus* and was a *Kirkus*, NPR, and *Quill & Quire* best middle-grade book of 2020, as well as a USBBY and Texas Lone Star selection. *The Great Bear*, the second book in The Misewa Saga series, is currently shortlisted for the Ontario Library Association's Silver Birch Award. A sought-after speaker and educator, and winner of the Writers' Union of Canada's Freedom to Read Award, Dave is a member of Norway House Cree Nation and currently lives in Winnipeg. For more information, visit his website: darobertson.ca and follow him on Twitter: @DaveAlexRoberts.